THE AMERICAN COLLECTION 7: THEIR SIN CITY SHOWGIRL

Dixie Lynn Dwyer

MENAGE EVERLASTING

Siren Publishing, Inc.
www.SirenPublishing.com

A SIREN PUBLISHING BOOK
IMPRINT: Ménage Everlasting

THE AMERICAN SOLDIER COLLECTION 7: THEIR SIN CITY
SHOWGIRL
Copyright © 2014 by Dixie Lynn Dwyer

ISBN: 978-1-62741-369-5

First Printing: June 2014

Cover design by Les Byerley
All art and logo copyright © 2014 by Siren Publishing, Inc.

ALL RIGHTS RESERVED: This literary work may not be
reproduced or transmitted in any form or by any means, including
electronic or photographic reproduction, in whole or in part, without
express written permission.

All characters and events in this book are fictitious. Any resemblance
to actual persons living or dead is strictly coincidental.

Printed in the U.S.A.

PUBLISHER
Siren Publishing, Inc.
www.SirenPublishing.com

DEDICATION

Dear Readers,

May you enjoy the latest addition to my American Soldier Collection.

Their Sin City Showgirl is a story about survival and learning to trust again.

Life has thrown J.J. some pretty difficult and frightful experiences, yet she trudges on, determined to be the strong, independent woman that has made her the best investigator and woman she can be.

Just as she feels like there's no hope of surviving, or getting out of the major trouble she is in, Conway, Brook, Lincoln, and Calder enter her life, and immediately thrust her into their own protective custody. She's keeping secrets. So are they. But she'll soon realize that they are more than just soldiers trying to do a job. Just as they realize she is more than some troubled woman on the run, with a bull's-eye on her forehead.

Sometimes, life's circumstances cause one's heart to close up, and forget how to love, how to trust, and to just feel. To learn to love again in little steps takes a higher power. To love for a minute, for an hour, for a day, may seem to be the most difficult task. And to learn to love for life may seem impossible.

Enjoy their journey.
Hugs,

~Dixie~

THE AMERICAN SOLDIER COLLECTION 7: THEIR SIN CITY SHOWGIRL

DIXIE LYNN DWYER
Copyright © 2014

Prologue

"Please. This is not why I took this job. I'm not interested in this. Please." Undercover Nevada State Police Detective, Marlee Davidson stated as she tried to undo the bindings on her wrists. In a flash, the tables had turned on her. There was no one around to call to for help. No one knew she was out at this hour. The lead she'd thought she had was a setup. That conniving little bitch, Tara, was part of this.

"Oh, you are interested. I can tell, and so can the others."

He caressed her hair. When he'd first approached she'd had to do a double take. Then, of course, came the realization that he may know who she was. But he didn't lead onto that. He toyed with her. She realized that this man was in fact a killer. She was shocked.

And she knew he was the killer because Tara had led her here. Marlee had thought that she was catching a break in the case. She'd figured out that whenever the McCues had a private party in the small back room of the casino, deals were going down. Men were placing their orders, but some big shots were fulfilling their fantasies.

She tried again unsuccessfully to pull her wrists from the bindings. It was no use. The fucker had gotten her. After years of training, working undercover, and finally proving to her commanders that she was capable of a mission like this, she'd fucked up.

The smack to the side of her head came out of nowhere, breaking her line of thought.

She gasped, and then sidestepped and tried to use her legs to defend herself.

"I thought you were special. When I saw you here, the new girl, the long red hair and pretty little figure, I knew I would have you. I planned this all out, ya know. The dim lights, the loud music. Now it's time to play the game. You're going to do exactly as I say. You're smart. I know you know how to improvise," he stated, and the expression on his face, and in his tone of voice, alerted her gut instincts immediately. Was her cover fully blown? Did he know she was working undercover. *Oh, fuck. What am I going to do?*

"No, I'm not going to do exactly what you say. I didn't sign up for this. It's not part of the job requirement working at the casino. Where's McCue? He won't let you do this," she said and he struck her again.

He grabbed her by the throat and stared into her face. She saw the evil, the hatred in his eyes, and knew she was going to die.

"You wanted to catch the men who are responsible for the missing women? It was your choice to come here. Now you're part of the show."

He ran his finger down the side of her cheek to her lips, as he held her neck with his other hand. She was pressed against the table, as the music got louder and the sounds of the drums and the bass made her entire body pulse.

Something changed in his eyes as he stared at her. Something evil, dark now attacked her senses. He quickly twisted her around and then stepped back.

"Dance for me, slut. Make up for me finding you here, in this club. I know you were going to cheat on me."

She was confused. She didn't understand what the hell he was saying. One second it sounded as if he knew she was working undercover, a cop on the case of the missing women, and the next, he was telling her to dance for him and make up for cheating on him. She was confused.

He slammed his fist down on top of her shoulder like a sledgehammer. She screamed, as she fell to her knees.

"That's right. This is where you belong." He shoved his palm against her forehead. The back of her head hit the lip of the table from the booth behind her.

He started to unzip his pants.

"No. No!" she screamed as she tried to stand up, despite the pain in her shoulder and the hinderance of the bindings on her wrists.

He struck her again.

She screamed.

He grabbed her by her hair and she was forced to look up into his evil eyes, as the music continued to fill the room. No one was coming. No one was going to stop him from fulfilling his fantasy. The lights flashed and shimmered around the room and across the ceiling. The setting was like a nightclub, with the blasting music, the pounding of the bass, the ultraviolet rays of light and flashes of white and silver pulsating around them. It made her feel frazzled, unable to focus.

"You chose to be here."

"No. I didn't. Let me go. People are looking for me. I was supposed to meet them," she screamed at him, as the flashes of white and silver light passed across his face. He appeared wild and angry. She attempted to stand up. He shoved her back down.

"Oh, you mean your fellow cops? Yeah, well, they'll meet up with you, very soon."

She swallowed hard. He knew she was a cop. Her cover was blown. But how? She had been so careful.

Tara?

She tried to escape on her knees, and as she fell to the floor face first, he grabbed her by her hair and pulled her back up. The pain radiated from her shoulders and neck to the roots of her hair. She screamed for help but knew she wouldn't be heard among the loud music, the wild and crazy flashing lights, and the bass of those damn drums. Her heart was pounding just as fast and fear consumed her. There was no escaping this man. She'd failed at her job. She'd failed and it was going to cost her her life.

He pulled her up and stared at her.

"They'll see you again. Your pig friends. At the crime scene," he whispered and then the expression on his face was so evil, so intense, she knew this was it.

"Fuck you. I know who you are. They'll figure it out, and then they'll kill you. Your people will find out what kind of sick bastard you really are."

A small smirk emerged on his face as he undid his zipper and dropped his pants.

"No. They won't."

* * * *

Julianna "J.J." Jacobs stole a peek at the crowd from behind the heavy, velvet, red stage curtain. A group of female performers covered the stage, each young woman dancing her heart out hoping to stand out from the others and catch her big break. The beat of the fast drums brought a feel of excitement and energy toward the crowd. The women danced their hearts out, keeping up with the fast beat and maintaining their form. The shiny sequin beaded skirts hugged their shapely hips, as the shimmering, beaded trims, whipped back and forth against their toned thighs. They looked fantastic as the women performed their number simultaneously with perfection just like during rehearsals this morning.

She stood backstage, waiting for her moment in the spotlight. Five nights a week and almost two months into this gig. She had to have established some credibility by now.

She looked around the room backstage. It was a madhouse, too. It had an area for makeup, one for hair, and another with floor-to-ceiling mirrors to practice routines and check yourself out from head to toe.

She couldn't help but feel a bit on edge. She wasn't nervous, but she knew that time was running out. A third woman had gone missing three days ago, and no one knew shit.

J.J. was trying her hardest to play her role and find out information. But with one of the women who'd disappeared being a federal agent, things were looking pretty bleak. There was no connection to the casino, but J.J. knew that's how these men got away with it. The victims always left the premises and then disappeared. Or at least that's what the detectives and the feds thought. The crime scenes were never anywhere in the vicinity of this club. But they'd caught a break. They'd received an anonymous call from someone who was approached to prostitute for money. She was scared, and she knew about the murders. Too bad they couldn't track her down now.

J.J. peeked out toward the crowd, knowing that she was to perform next. She wasn't really nervous. She just wanted to be certain to pull off her act. Things were getting complicated around here. Three weeks, and numerous conversations with fellow employees, as well as the bosses, and she didn't have enough evidence to point fingers. All she had to go by were her gut instincts. Being a cop, she relied on those on a daily basis.

She didn't want to blow her cover, but she also was desperate for answers and wanted to nail the scumbag behind the multiple murders. Two federal agents had disappeared, Meredith Perkins and Denise Sinclair, just three days ago. Before that the total was five, including J.J.'s friend and fellow undercover officer, Marlee Davidson. The Commander wanted to pull her out, but she'd begged him to let her remain just for a little while longer. Marlee's murder hit the department hard. She was young, beautiful, and establishing her abilities as an undercover detective. But the risks with this case were higher than most. Her cover had been blown. They knew that because the prick responsible for killing her left her real name and her police badge number on a piece of paper on top of her body. It was like a laugh-in-your-face type of message. He was letting them know that he felt smarter and brazen enough to get away with this.

Her commander didn't want to put J.J. in. Commander Frank Reynolds was a good friend. He was a man she trusted her life with, and he of course took on that role after she'd lost her fiancé, Anthony, to the job. His nephew, Anthony, was killed in the line of duty, during an undercover operation. The details were still shady, but there was nothing any of them could do about it. Case closed, and Anthony was dead.

J.J. swallowed hard. That had been two years ago, and she hadn't had a relationship with any man since. She probably never would. Her life was law enforcement.

She looked around the room behind her. No one was paying her any attention right now. It seemed that whenever someone was up next to perform, they stayed clear of them. They gave them time to do their rituals or whatever they needed to do to prepare mentally for the performance. So in the downtime J.J. thought about how she'd gotten here, and how badly she wanted to solve the case and catch this bastard.

In her mind she thought back about the private meeting in her commander's office. The one where FBI agents were present to ask for assistance because they needed a certain undercover female officer with a specific look, as well as capabilities.

J.J. figured not many cops had natural talent. Talent that could land them record deals, or even acting jobs. That wasn't for J.J. Well, at least she hadn't considered it until Anthony suggested it to her one night. They'd talked about their future, about getting married, and about her safety. She was always a bit on the wild side. Growing up watching *Dirty Harry* movies with her father, and even *Die Hard* movies, enticed her into getting involved with law enforcement. It was in her blood. Her father had died on the job, and more than likely she would, too.

She sighed as she looked out toward the crowd, taking a peek from the curtain. She wondered if the McCues were there yet. She needed to get some evidence, and find out if there was an illegal prostitution business going on, and if Marlee's cover had been exposed because she'd confided in one of the other dancers to get information. A lot was riding on tonight.

She thought about the meeting at Commander Reynolds's office.

"It's a dangerous situation, J.J. I really don't feel comfortable placing you in there, but you fit the part." She stood there with her hands by her sides, as the other detectives and some big shot from the FBI looked her body over.

"I know. I get it," she replied. Her large breasts, voluptuous figure, and experience with both singing and dancing set her apart from the others. But she had her own reasons for wanting this job. Marlee. She was an old friend, a fellow undercover detective working the case from the start, and the third victim to this violence. Beaten, raped, tortured, and then murdered, J.J. was out for justice, big time. She lived for shit like this. She knew she lived life on the edge after losing Anthony. It was all worth it, if she could stop the killer or killers and save some lives.

"We can't secure more than three people on the inside. The Emerald City Casino is like Fort Knox. You'll be on your own, except for the aid of the camera in the elevator in the left wing, the hallway outside of McCue's private suite, and the back entrance through the kitchen exit in the corner lot. If you're in any trouble in those locations, we have men inside who will see you and move in," her commander, Reynolds, stated.

"Anywhere else, and you're on your own," the FBI agent added.

She nodded her head in agreement. Everyone was talking about the murders. Congressman Dooley had even spoken about it during one of his campaigns. Not that she like that guy. He kind of gave her the creeps, but he seemed to be trying to inform the public and also give support to the police department. The man had ties everywhere, and would surely get reelected.

"If at any point, you feel that your cover has been blown, J.J., I want you out of there." She nodded her head at the Commander. Justice would be served.

J.J. took a deep breath and released it. She worked for the Nevada State Police, enrolled in the academy at twenty years old, and by twenty-two she'd made their special investigations unit. That was four years ago. Anthony had taught her a lot. He gave her the extra training to keep her safe, and make her have the tools necessary to keep alive. It's how they'd fallen in love. She was good at what she did and she was tough. But knowing that the people responsible for these murders were somewhere out there in the crowd tonight made her belly tighten.

She felt the hand on her shoulder and abruptly turned around, ready to pounce.

"Whoa! Holy shit, are you okay, Jade?" Tara asked, taking a step back. She was a fellow dancer, involved in the belly dancing act going on after J.J.'s solo. She also was tight with the McCues, and J.J. didn't trust her.

J.J. shook her head, feigning embarrassment, but really it just showed how on edge she was. It seemed to her that every natural response was an opportunity to get information. She was getting used to her fake name, too. Jade was kind of cool for a fake name. But considering how green her eyes were, everyone told her it was the perfect name for her.

"I'm sorry. I guess I'm just a little nervous," she whispered, and then took advantage of Tara's approach. Tara had mentioned making some extra money just a few days ago. She was hinting around J.J. to see if she was hard for cash. Knowing how the FBI believed that the cases had something to do with prostitution, she thought she would take the bait and play up to Tara to see if this was an in.

"I totally need to focus. I can't fuck this up. I need this job," J.J. stated and then swallowed hard before looking back toward the stage curtain.

"Money's tight, huh?" Tara asked.

"Tight? Shit, I'm behind on my rent. I'm avoiding the landlord until Friday, payday, then half will go to the rent and some of the other bills. I'll be lucky if I'll have enough for one regular meal after that."

Tara smiled and then she rubbed her arm.

"Listen, after your act, come talk to me. I've got an in on some special side work. It's a bit wild, kind of kinky, but the pay is fantastic. Plus, with your great looks and body, you could be very busy in the extra activities," Tara said with a wink. J.J. lowered her voice and inched closer.

"Are you talking about prostitution?"

Tara looked around them.

"Listen, it's not that bad, and the guys are really wealthy, powerful men. They pay big bucks."

She pretended to think about that a moment.

"What kind of kinky stuff would I have to do?"

"We'll talk more after the show. If you're interested, I'll give you the lowdown, but you better not say a word to any of the other girls. I could get into a lot of trouble even speaking about it to you."

"Trouble with who, like a pimp?"

Tara chuckled.

"I don't think Dexter, Martin, or Prentice would like being called pimps." Tara chuckled as J.J. nearly gasped aloud. Martin, Dexter, and Prentice were the owners of the casino. Dexter and Martin were brothers, and they were dangerous, and Prentice was a nasty, steroid head. The man got angry at the drop of a hat, and she had seen his rage. This was definitely useful information.

"Jade, you're on in five," one of the stagehands said, as the music to her number began softly in the background, as the MC got the crowd warmed up before he introduced her. She adjusted her breasts in the two-sizes-too-small sequin dress she wore and gave a little exhale of nerves. J.J. was five foot six without the outrageous heels and was well-endowed, a bit too well-endowed for the dress she wore tonight, but this was Vegas and she was a Vegas showgirl.

She wore her brown hair up high on her head in some fancy hairstyle she would have never dreamed of trying to recreate herself. The beauticians and makeup artists took care of everything backstage, and when J.J. looked at herself in the mirror even she was amazed.

There were numerous beaded clips and accent pieces scattered around the hairdo. The makeup artist had attached false eyelashes, which made J.J.'s deep jade green eyes stand out even more.

This afternoon when she had met Dexter McCue he had complimented her on them and she hoped his flirtatious advances would land her the opportunity to get some inside information.

"You're on. Break a leg, doll," the stagehand said with a wink, as the curtain parted and the crowd began to cheer. She was in her role as a Vegas showgirl, and it was time to snag the attention of the bad guys.

* * * *

Martin and Dexter McCue sat down in the booth to the right of the stage. They had a perfect view of the audience as well as the stage. Martin's brother, Dexter, had had his eye on Jade for the past two weeks, but so had Martin. She was a knockout, with a body of a porn star, and the voice of a fucking angel. They had both received numerous requests from clients to have her. But one glance at Dexter, and both Martin and Prentice knew he wanted her for himself.

However, Prentice found out that Jade had been asking some questions around the club. The last bitch that had asked a bunch of questions turned out to be a federal agent. That was a huge fucking mess for Prentice and him to handle.

There were ways to see if this woman was on the up-and-up. And because Martin had such the creative mind, he'd come up with a great plan. If all went well, Dexter would own her by the end of the night. If not, then the songbird would be dead.

He turned his attention toward the stage, Jade's voice pulling him from his morbid plans. Yeah, the woman was perfect.

She had an amazing voice, and she moved her body in such a way, not a man in the place was unaffected. The shape of her hips, the swell of her large breasts, was all-appealing to the eyes. From this distance, Martin couldn't see her gorgeous green eyes, but he knew they were bold and mesmerizing.

His dick instantly hardened. She could be the perfect match for those special clients of his. If he paired Jade up with Tara and Caitlin, it could be the easiest hundred grand he ever made. Martin would see what his client thought about the two other women he'd secured for him. The meet and greet would take place in Jade's presence, and then Martin could speak to her about joining in and making some cash. But first, he would have a taste of her.

"What's that look for? Are you planning something?" Dexter asked Martin.

"Brother, don't you worry. Tonight might turn into a very special night for us." He looked back at Jade as she belted out a high note that sent the crowd cheering. She was fucking impressive. So much so that he would consider keeping her as his regular fuck. His brother might want her too, but he'd handle that. She was that fucking special. Martin imagined her tied to his bed, kneeling on the floor in front of him, calling him master and sir. *Holy fuck. I want her. I'm going to have her. She'll accept. She has to.*

* * * *

J.J. was backstage standing behind the dressing curtain when Tara approached.

"Don't bother with that one. Wear this one," she said, and then handed her a very sleek black dress that dipped low in the front and the back. Her breasts would barely be covered.

J.J. placed her hands on her hips and stared at Tara with an expression she hoped signified her displeasure.

"Are you kidding me? That dress is not made for a woman with my figure." She placed it back onto the rack and to the other side of the changing curtain.

"You have to wear it. With these heels. I believe you're a size seven." She handed her very high heels, practically stilettos.

"Why do I have to wear this?" she asked.

Tara looked around and then moved closer.

"Martin wants you to wear this. He asked that you join him and his brother for dinner and a private party in the back room."

"A private party? Hey, I didn't say that I wanted to get involved in what you mentioned earlier. I've never done anything like that before. I don't know if I—"

Tara raised her hand up for J.J. to stop talking. "I know that. He has been watching you. Men have been requesting you. Now is the opportunity for you to ask him questions, see what this type of work is all about, and then make a decision." Tara took a deep breath and released it.

"But I can tell you right now, there's no declining Martin's offer, whatever it is. He has been paying close attention to you. He's interested."

"But I may not be," J.J. said, as she was trying to come up with a plan to notify the guys who were supposed to be watching her.

"He won't hurt you. If you're submissive, like you seem you would be in bed, then you'll be just fine, and it won't hurt too badly."

"Submissive? Me? Hurt too badly? Oh God, what is going to happen?"

"It's really not that bad. Prentice is the one to worry about. If he takes an interest in you...just avoid Prentice at all costs. Now hurry up. I am supposed to bring you there. I'm on for tonight, too, along with Caitlin," Tara said.

J.J. stared at the black dress. When she placed it on, she looked at herself in the mirror.

Holy shit. This is definitely not me. There's no place to put a gun, a knife, or anything as a weapon.

She thought about it, grabbed the black purse, and then looked around before reaching into her backpack and pulling out her switchblade. It was better than walking into something like this completely naked. Although that was exactly how she felt.

* * * *

"You sneaky son of a bitch. What are you up to?" Dexter asked his brother, Martin, as Jade entered the room. His heart was pounding inside of his chest. His cock was so fucking hard, it was difficult to breathe. He wanted this woman. Had obsessed over her the last two weeks. His brother knew that he was interested. Was he offering her to him?

"Is she mine, Martin?" he whispered, not taking his eyes off of her.

"Not yet. Let's see how this plays out. I got dibs first, and if she's as perfect as I think she'll be, then we'll discuss sharing her."

"Fuck, yeah. I'm in," Dexter said as he rubbed his hands together and watched her approach. She was with Tara, and Caitlin immediately made her way over to their special guest's private booth. There were only a few other couples around. Prentice sat at a table, and made the connections between the men who ordered a woman or two for the night and the right woman to meet their needs and taste.

To anyone else, it would look like a social gathering. The women never left the room with the men. They met up elsewhere, whether in a hotel room upstairs, or in another venue nearby. It all depended upon the request.

"Sir, shall I go introduce myself to our guest?" Tara asked, as she bowed her head and waited for her orders.

Dexter took her hand and brought it to his lips. He kissed the top of it and Tara smiled as she looked up, but kept her head bowed.

"You look stunning, Tara. Please make sure that you and Caitlin do your best to please our guest. He's a platinum member, after all." He kissed her hand and then released it. Tara bowed at Martin and Martin gave her a wink. She went on her way.

Dexter and Martin both stood up from the table to greet Jade.

"Thank you for joining us this evening, Jade," Martin said, and then took her hand and brought it to his lips. He kissed her knuckles and breathed in her perfume.

Dexter felt his stomach tighten. He felt hungry, and in his mind he imagined ripping that dress from Jade's body and exploring her thoroughly. Especially her large breasts. It appeared as if the material was about to part and reveal exactly what he wanted to see. He licked his lips. She seemed to blush. *She's fucking perfect.*

He hoped that she denied his brother's requests. He would get much pleasure out of forcing her to do what he wanted. He loved rough sex.

"Thank you for inviting me. I'm starving," she added so sweetly, and Dexter snapped his fingers as Martin motioned for her to take a seat in the large, custom booth.

As she slid along to the back, her breasts moved and swayed, nearly popping from the material hanging there. She immediately placed her hand over the spot, denying him the simple pleasure of seeing more of her flesh. She'd pay for that, and every little naughty thing she did that he felt was punishable. He shivered with anticipation.

Martin took position on one side of her and Dexter slid in to take position on her other side. It was time to let his brother lead, and hopefully the night would end with her between them in bed.

* * * *

J.J. took in her surroundings, and of course her gut instincts were in overdrive. This wasn't right. She was too exposed like this. She denied the feelings, blaming it on the dress she wore, and the fact that she sat between two very large, resourceful men who were more than likely killers. She swallowed hard.

"Champagne or wine?" Martin asked.

"Oh, sir, whatever you would like," she said and his eyes instantly sparkled. A small smirk hit his lips and she felt that instant concern hit her. Did she say something that would entice him?

"You are so very beautiful, Jade. Your voice, your performance tonight, every night, is amazing. You have pleased us both," Dexter said, and then he lifted his hand to her face, as he turned in his seat to face her. He rubbed his thumb gently against her ear, and lobe, making the small dangling earring move.

"Thank you, sir. I've been trying very hard."

"And it shows, Jade," Martin said as the waiter appeared and poured them three glasses of champagne. She watched him carefully, being sure that nothing was placed into the glass. She watched the bottle pop open, and then stared as the waiter poured the glasses. Martin handed her one glass, and they both took their own glasses.

"To new beginnings and adventures," Martin whispered, holding her gaze.

"To undeniable pleasure," Dexter added, and she looked at him and then swallowed hard before taking a sip from her glass as they had from theirs.

The waiter returned with a tray of appetizers. Shrimp, toasted bread with sundried tomato and crumbled goat cheese, fried oysters, and some caviar.

Martin took one of the shrimps, dipped it into sauce, and then moved it toward her in offering.

She slowly opened her mouth, and he held the shrimp there, with his other hand cupped next to her chin underneath. She went to eat the shrimp, but he held on to the tail, making her pull harder.

"Come here," he whispered as she swallowed the shrimp. He was going to kiss her, and she didn't think that was a great idea. Not with the sounds that were coming from across the room. Tara was making out with some man. She was straddling his waist and he was grabbing at her.

"Focus on me. Taking orders is important."

"Orders?" she whispered.

Martin grabbed her face and kissed her hard on the mouth. She struggled a moment, but just as quickly as he kissed her, he released her.

Dexter grabbed a hold of her hair from behind her head and forced her to look at him.

"Tara said that you may be interested in making some extra money."

She shook her head in denial.

"No, Tara lied?" he asked, with an expression that warned her that he was a psycho. He looked so out of it, almost high on something.

"What did Tara tell you?"

"She didn't say much, just that I could make some extra money if I wanted to."

"And you didn't ask what you would need to do?" Martin asked her.

"She told me that she would explain tonight. I don't understand what's going on here. Why are you holding me like this?" she asked, glancing toward Dexter.

"Because you're going to be ours. We've decided," Dexter said, and then moved his hand along her leg, pressing his hand between her thighs.

She gasped and began to move, trying to get out of his grasp, but now Martin grabbed her hand. He used one to press her thigh wider, as his brother pressed her other thigh wider. His other hand placed her hand over his crotch and she felt his huge erection.

"No. Please, I don't want this," she stated, as she tried to figure out a way to get out of this situation. But then her attention, and theirs, was brought toward the doorway. Someone burst into the room. He was dressed in black. He approached the table where Tara was straddling the other man.

"You cheating little bitch!" the man in black yelled. J.J. jerked, but Martin and Dexter kept her in place. She felt Martin's cock grow larger. He was getting off on watching this. *What in God's name is going on?*

In a flash the man in black pulled Tara from the man she straddled. The man punched the other man, sending him falling to the ground. That man got up and moved out of the way.

Jade felt her stomach twist and turn. Then she gasped as the man in black struck Tara, grabbed her around the waist, and bent her over the table.

"Oh, my God, we have to stop him. He's going to hurt her," J.J. stated.

"Are you scared?" Dexter asked.

"Yes," J.J. replied.

"Pay attention. Do you think that we would allow just any man to come in here and do that to one of our girls?" Dexter asked.

"Quiet, he's getting to the best part," Martin exclaimed.

J.J. watched as the man in black yelled at Tara.

"Do you want me or do you want him?" he asked in a roar.

"You. I want you. You're so strong and forceful. I want it hard and fast," Tara yelled back at him.

"Oh, my God," J.J. whispered, as she realized what exactly was happening here. This was a setup. Had they staged this to get her reaction?" she wondered, but as she stared at Tara being taken by the man in black, she realized that it was really happening.

Dexter stroked his fingers over her covered pussy.

"Are you wet, Jade? Did that turn you on as much as it turned me on?"

She shook her head.

"No. I don't want this. I won't do that," she whispered.

"Don't be rash. Give it some time to sink in," Martin said as he pressed her hands up and down over his shaft. Despite the pants he wore she could feel his hard erection. This was really bad. She needed to think quickly and get the hell out of here.

"It's all a game. The clients have all different types of requests. Some want to dominate and feel in charge, while others want to be taken charge of," Dexter said still gliding his hand up and down the inside of her thigh. Tara was moaning and crying in the distance. It made J.J. feel sick. How could she want that? How could Tara and these other women accept such treatment? Were they so desperate for money that they would allow men to do that?

"He's hurting her."

Martin grabbed her face and cupped her cheek. She was grateful he no longer had a hand between her legs. She crossed her legs immediately blocking off Dexter's touch.

"Sometimes pleasing the client means pain. Don't you like pain?" he asked her. *The sick fuck.*

Every instinct in her body wanted to lash out at this piece of shit, but she couldn't. She didn't want to blow her cover.

"Pain? They beat them?" she asked.

"Sometimes, or if the woman doesn't do what is asked completely, she suffers the greatest amounts of pain," Dexter stated.

Martin released her face.

"You have a lot to think about. But don't believe for one moment that we would send you to the wolves without training," Martin said.

"I'm not interested." He released her hand and stared straight ahead.

"You will be. I'd hate to have to kill you," he stated very seriously and without taking his eyes off of Tara.

J.J. heard the scream and then the sound of something banging. She jerked up, not remotely close to being over Martin's statement and threat of killing her, to see Tara's head being smashed against the table.

"Prentice!" Martin yelled out. Prentice immediately headed toward Tara and the man in black who was thrusting into Tara from behind while he beat her. J.J. closed her eyes and felt her body shaking. Tara was going to die right here in front of her.

"Let me up. I can't watch this." J.J. raised her voice as Martin stood up, just as Prentice pulled the man in black off of Tara. J.J. saw his face and had to hide her gasp. *Congressman Dooley? Holy fuck. Oh, shit. Oh, God, no. This is really bad.*

She turned away, uncertain if the man would recognize her or not. He had been so involved in pushing information onto the public about the case. He could easily have gotten information on the investigation and the undercover operation.

Oh, God, *no. Oh, God, he probably knew about Marlee and Denise. Marlee knew Dooley. He was up for reelection. Everyone wanted to elect him. He was for the cops, the first responders, and for military. Oh God. No one would believe this.*

"Jade, darling. Are you okay?" Dexter asked, wrapping an arm around her waist. She felt him thrust his cock against her from behind. She was nearly against the table. His mouth was on her neck, and she thought he was going to try to rape her.

She pulled from his grasp.

"I'm going to be sick. I need a restroom," she stated.

"Take her, Dexter. Then bring her to our room. There's no need to waste time pondering over her choice. After watching that scene unfold, I've got some things I'd like to try on our little songbird."

She knew what things he wanted to do. She'd just witnessed a sexual assault. Even though Tara had claimed to want it, and had allowed it, it was still a crime. She was nearly beaten to death.

"Martin. We have a problem," Prentice stated. She turned to look, along with Martin and Dexter, who had his hand on her shoulder.

"What's the fucking problem?" he asked.

Congressman Dooley downed a drink as he pulled up his fly and stared straight ahead. He saw her. Would he remember who she was?

"I think you owe me, McCue. She didn't do a good job fulfilling my fantasy. How about that one?" he yelled from across the room and stared at J.J.

J.J. took a quick glance behind him. Tara lay motionless on the floor, blood dripping from her temple, dress ripped, mouth bloodied. She thought about the pictures from the crime scenes of the other victims. These men were a bunch of rapists and murderers. How many more were out there? How many women were still missing? The rage, the anger was becoming too much to bury.

As she looked up, the congressman was approaching. "I need the ladies' room," she said and Dexter pulled her closer.

"Wait. Let me see her. She's got the tits I wanted. Look at those fuckers. She'd be perfect," he said and then stopped a few feet in front of her as Martin placed his hand up for the congressman to halt.

"Martin. Tara isn't breathing," Prentice yelled out.

J.J. was shocked, and looked toward Martin and the congressman stared at her.

"I've seen you before," he stated.

She needed to think quickly and get out of there. Tara was possibly dead, murdered.

"She's in the show. She's one of the best acts we got," Dexter said as he held her from behind and then cupped her breast. She kept her face away from the congressman. If he identified her, she was dead. She remembered her switchblade, and reached into her purse even though all she wanted to do was to push Dexter's grimy hands off her breast. "They feel nice, I bet. Are they real?" the congressman asked.

You are so fucking dead. You're over, Dooley. You rotten, no good son of a bitch.

Martin was walking toward Tara.

"I need to go," J.J. whispered as she leaned her head back against Dexter's shoulder, giving him better access to her breast. Anything to get out of here, get to her commander, and blow this fucking case wide open.

"I bet she could take both of us. I'll pay for her, like I did the others," Dooley whispered and then reached over to stroke her other breast. She turned into Dexter's arms, her hand on the switchblade.

"We'll think about it. She's ours tonight," Dexter said as he held her tight.

"Wait, I've seen her somewhere before. It's not from the show."

J.J. panicked and pretended to gag as if she were about to puke. "Oh, shit. I have to get her to the ladies' room. Go over there. It's going to cost you for us to get rid of the body."

"I'll pay, just like I did for the others," Congressman Dooley stated.

J.J. struggled to get away from Dexter and run to the bathroom, but he wouldn't release her. She glanced over her shoulder and saw Dooley in a dead stare at her. His eyes widened and he started to head toward Martin.

The door to the bathroom was straight ahead, and the exit right near there.

Dexter rushed her ahead, and she made her move. She stomped on his foot, shoved her elbow into his stomach, and ran for the exit door. "Stop!" Dexter yelled as he followed, coughing from her elbow shot. She shoved open the door and an alarm blared, as Martin and Prentice came running out of the first room.

"Stop her, Dexter. She's a fucking cop."

She ran through the parking lot. No one was coming. She was on her own. Obviously the cameras didn't work. There was only the one in the back of the building through the kitchen exit. She was nowhere near that side of the building. She lowered down near a set of cars, and tried to catch her breath. She pulled off the high heels and threw them underneath the car. She looked around, and didn't hear a sound. She could hail a cab, if she could get through the parking lot and into the front of the building. She started to run when she felt a hand on her shoulder pull her back down. As she turned around, Dexter punched her in the face. She gripped the switchblade and held on as he continued to try and hurt her and stop her from going anywhere.

His hands were on her throat.

"You fucking bitch. You're a fucking cop? I wanted you. We would have been great together. I'm going to kill you. But first, we're going to show you what we do to cop bitches."

She was kicking him and he shoved her against the hood of the car. She couldn't breathe and with her only defense in hand, she stuck him in the side with the knife. He let go, she coughed and cried out, and then kicked him in the stomach. He was holding his side with one hand and used his other to reach out and grip the material of her dress. She slammed her knee up hard and fast, connecting with his chin and nose, splattering blood everywhere. He yelled out and she decked him in the face. He fell backward onto the ground.

She was panting for air, shaking with fury and fear.

She could hear yelling, and saw security running through the parking lot looking for her. There was no one to trust, just the three security guys placed there undercover, and she didn't know who they were.

She scrambled to get out of there. She ran as fast as she could and down the Las Vegas strip, away from the killers and into the crowd of crazies. A glance over her shoulder and her peripheral vision caught sight of the entourage of black-tinted vehicles. The congressman's private security team. She was in seriously heavy shit, and no one could be trusted. It was two o'clock in the morning. She needed to get to her commander.

Hailing a cab, she jumped in and gave the address of the safe house. She looked behind her and saw no indication that she was being followed. Her cheek throbbed something terrible, as well as her throat, her arms, and back. She would be covered in bruises, but it was better than being dead.

This was a major clusterfuck, and she was caught in the middle. As the cab driver drove her to the destination, she thought about the events that had unfolded and the situation as a whole. She'd nearly died tonight, and deep down she knew that things were going to get worse before they got better.

Congressman Dooley is a killer. He just killed Tara, and I heard him say he would pay for Martin and Dexter to get rid of her body just like he did for the others. He was at the heart of this. Everyone adored him. What would the FBI do when they found out? Are they going to believe me? Oh God, he killed her. I'm a witness to a murder, and the killer is Congressman Dooley.

Chapter 1

"This sounds like a bad fucking situation," Sandman stated.

Commander Frank Reynolds ran his hand across his whiskers. He was speaking on a secure line. He couldn't believe that this case had turned into this. There were few people to trust, and neither him nor J.J. felt confident about the witness protection program since her life had been threatened repeatedly, and he was asked to turn his back and let her get killed. He was sick with worry. He'd promised Anthony that he would take care of J.J. But this was beyond his means.

"I wouldn't have called you like this if it wasn't a last resort. It is a fucking bad situation. There are only a few individuals I can trust. They're working on gathering evidence and making sure that the person responsible will not get off on some bullshit mistake. It's going to take some time. She's in serious danger. The threats are coming from more than capable sources. She's survived three attempts already. She's lucky to still be alive."

"I understand. I do this thing on the down low, so I get that we need to keep it under the radar. Are we talking feds only?"

"Politics, too."

"Fuck. That's why I hate fucking politics. If people just got their heads out of their asses and did the right thing, we wouldn't have half the fucking problems."

"Hey, Sandman, you don't need to tell me. I've learned that people aren't always who they say they are. I trust you, because Anthony always did."

"Anthony was a good man. So what can you tell me about this woman?" Sandman asked.

"Not a lot. I think that's better for your safety and for hers. I need her placed somewhere she won't be noticed or recognized. Your town is filled with retired military. There have to be some more highly trained protectors available."

"You're seriously going to leave me with squat on this woman? No details on the case? Her involvement or professional position? Is she going to be a pain in the ass or something?"

Frank chuckled.

"J.J. is tough. She's resourceful and she's not too keen on this present idea of mine, however, keeping that pretty little head of hers intact is my number one priority. Sandman…she went through some heavy shit. She's a bundle of nerves. What she went through was pretty damn traumatic. She knows that her life is in jeopardy, and she's pissed off, too. I have nowhere else to turn, and I made a promise to myself, for Anthony's sake, to keep watch over her."

"She was involved with Anthony?" Sandman asked.

"They got engaged two weeks before he died."

"Shit. I'm sorry, Frank. I had no idea that Anthony was even seeing anyone."

"They were keeping it under the radar. She was one of his trainees."

"Oh, shit, that must have been interesting."

"You have no idea. Anyway. I can have her out there within the week. I just need to secure a plan, so she's not followed."

"Let me help with that. I already have a place and some men in mind. I'll call you on this line within the hour."

"Great. Thank you, Sandman. I'll keep you posted on what's going on over here. Hey, if something happens to me—"

"Nothing is going to happen to you."

"If something happens to me, please, keep J.J. safe. She busted this case wide open. She's a hero, and she deserves to survive this."

* * * *

Sandman disconnected the call and swiveled around in his chair. He disconnected the wire that blocked anyone from tapping the call. He lived for shit like this still. He felt badly for this situation and for Frank and this woman. He had to be sure to take the necessary precautions and then some. If this case involved the feds, a politician, and some dirty shit, then this woman could already be as good as dead. He had to help Frank, keep his friends safe, too, and hope that they would take on this situation.

Conway, Brook, Calder, and Lincoln were tough sons of bitches. They were into some crazy shit, like creating high-tech bombs that weren't easily detected, and super crazy spy stuff. They did it for fun. Then, of course, were their real jobs as combat trainers, and Conway was the chief of police in town. Their land was out in the middle of nowhere, and totally secured with high-tech surveillance they created and fooled around with. They had enough guns and ammo to start and finish their own war. The more he thought about them, the more Sandman knew they were the best choice to keep this woman safe. He picked up the phone. Now if only he could convince them that their services were needed.

Chapter 2

J.J. sat straight-faced in the large black pickup truck, with tinted windows, alongside some big-ass agent and friend of Frank's. He was like six feet fucking four, had huge muscles, and looked experienced. She held her breath a few times, trying to stop her body from shaking. She had no control over it and it appeared to be getting worse. Of course she hadn't confided in Frank about it. He would worry more than he already worried.

She picked up the file he'd given her. At least Frank had informed this guy that she was more than capable of handling herself and that she wanted details on these men who were to be protecting her. She hated looking at this situation as needing protection, but after her small little house was blown up and her bank accounts raided, she knew she needed help. The kind of help that only Frank seemed to be able to get her. She was grateful. After all, if Dooley or his thugs got a hold of her first, she would experience the type of death she had only nightmares about. Now that was something else plaguing her. The nightmares. Waking up in a cold sweat, running for her life, and being caught by the McCues, Prentice, or Dooley himself. Their attack on her body was so surreal, it made her sleepless, with her revolver tucked under her pillow, and others scattered around the room.

She hoped that Frank's friend kept his promise about not informing these men of her professional status. Let them think she was weak and incapable. Then when they tried something, she would show them just how incapable she was.

She shook the thoughts from her head. Her new way of thinking was frightening her. She was combative and aggressive, even in thought. She was ready to fight, verbally or physically. This wasn't her. Sure she was tough, but bitchy, combative? Never. Not unless provoked. But considering the circumstances, she was beyond provoked. She was scared shitless, she felt out of control, completely alone, and distrusting with a vengeance.

"We'll be there in five minutes. I know their place is out there in the middle of nowhere, but they are very capable men. Their security is impeccable, and they know their shit. You'll be safe with them," Sandman stated.

"We'll see," she replied, and he looked her over and she pulled her sweater tighter against her chest. She wore high-collared shirts and sweaters to hide all the bruising. Dexter had done a number on her. She hadn't even remembered most of the fight. Just that her life depended on getting away from him. *Too bad the motherfucker hadn't died from the stab wound.*

That was another thing that really bothered her now. She didn't like men staring at her body. She felt exposed, vulnerable, even though she hadn't been raped. She supposed that it was from the way Dexter and Martin had touched her, forced her legs apart as they'd made her watch Tara play her role. Then of course Dexter fondled her breast as she let him in order to get free. Dooley did too. That piece of scum. She shivered from her thoughts. He wouldn't get away with this. He couldn't. He'd killed those women, and the McCues and Prentice had helped.

"Are you okay?" Sandman asked. She looked at him, wondering what he was talking about. Had she actually lost track of her thoughts? She realized the truck had stopped, and that she hadn't even noticed she was so lost.

"Fine," she said, holding the files to her chest, as she looked out the truck window. That's when she saw the chief of police truck, and the uniformed man standing outside of it. He looked different from in the picture. Conway Lewis was big and mean looking, and he reminded her of Anthony. Her guard went up another notch, as if that were even possible at this point.

* * * *

"Holy shit. This is the woman in danger?" Brook Lewis asked Calder Murphy as they zoomed in on her as she stepped out of the truck. They were inside the house, tweaking their outside perimeter cameras. As Sandman pulled onto the main dirt road leading up to their property and home, they were all fully aware of the visitors coming. Having the surveillance cameras and the underwire security throughout their property, every dwelling including their house, made each of them feel secure. It helped to handle the paranoia they still had four years after retiring from the service. Each of them had their own way of dealing with their readaptation to society. Protecting innocent people from harm on a down-low basis helped to feed the need inside of them to protect and serve. Of course Conway lived to protect and serve, so being the chief of police kept him calm. He was typical of a chief with his hard expression, intimidating size, take-no-shit attitude, and he barely smiled. People feared him, and that kept the town and the surrounding areas safe.

"She's young," Calder mumbled, zooming in on her face. He must have seen the bruise and gash to her cheek immediately as she got out of the truck, just as Brook had.

"Damn, that looks like it hurts," Brook added, feeling his gut clench. He hated to see women get smacked around. He had no tolerance for a man who could strike a woman or treat her badly. Nor did his buddies. Conway, especially, had no tolerance for it. He was called out on a few domestic violence calls outside of town, and he made sure to put the fear of God inside those men.

Calder pulled back slightly, to zero in on the rest of her, including her expression as Conway was introduced by Sandman.

"She looks untrusting," Brook stated.

"She looks pissed off and her eyes are darting around to everywhere else but to Conway. She's hiding something."

"So what else is new? You know how this shit goes down. We don't get much info at first, and then we use our skills to interrogate. She's probably just scared. Sandman said this situation requires special care. Her whereabouts had to remain hidden."

"Well then you two should check over the security system again before dinner. I've got the stew cooking and the guest bedroom all made up and ready. I want you to be sure to block out the cameras in her bedroom," Lincoln stated from the doorway. Their buddy was six feet three with blond crew cut hair, and tattoos up and down his forearms. He was well organized and on guard all the time. The man hardly ever slept, just like Calder.

"We did, but we kept the ones on her window so we could also set the motion sensors outside. Anyone comes out of that window or makes it far enough to climb into that window, and we'll all know it," Calder stated.

"Good. Then let's go meet our new houseguest," Lincoln said and then left the room. Brook glanced back at the flat screen television sets. The woman, their guest, was stunning, despite the look of fear in her eyes, and the way she constantly looked around her, ready to bolt. Something told Brook that this was going to be complicated. So why was he feeling a hint of interest and excitement as he headed out to the living room to meet her?

* * * *

J.J. looked around the living room as Conway gave her the tour. The man was so tall and big, he had to duck under the entryways throughout the home. As they entered through the kitchen, she could smell something delicious cooking on the stove in a huge pot. Her stomach rumbled and she swallowed hard. It had been days since she'd eaten a meal. Sure she picked at a few sandwiches, but since that night at the Emerald City Casino, she hadn't had much of an appetite. She'd lost some weight, but worked out harder than ever. She hoped she could continue the working out, even if she had to improvise on things to use for weights. The Conway guy seemed really fit, and was filled with muscles. People worked for bodies like his. Maybe there was a home gym or at minimum some weights to use.

He led her out to the living room, where three other men waited for them. She stopped short. Sandman nearly walked into her, and as he placed his hands on her shoulders, she sidestepped out of the way of his touch and nearly tripped. She must have looked like some crazy woman, but as she looked at them, prepared to retort viciously if necessary, none of them said a word. Their eyes only slightly changed, almost unnoticeably. But she noticed. She'd trained herself well. It was what made her a good undercover officer, and what also landed her in the middle of this mess.

"My fault. Please, meet the rest of the team. This is Brook Lewis, Calder Murphy, and Lincoln Jones," Sandman said as he pointed out each man. Brook nodded his head in a polite gesture to say hello. He probably realized he shouldn't put out his hand for her to shake. He feared it would get bitten off. *God, I feel like a caged animal. I'm so on edge.*

She nodded her head as she crossed her arms and looked around the room to avoid eye contact. That was so unlike her.

"Well, I'm sure you'll get better acquainted over dinner. Is that stew you're making, Lincoln?" Sandman asked.

J.J. wondered if he was the only one who cooked. She should offer to lend a hand. It was what she normally would do when she came to someone's home. But this wasn't normal. This was a sentence. All because of what she'd witnessed and who was responsible.

"It sure is. Want to stay and join us?" Lincoln asked.

"Sorry. I wish I could but Grace made some plans, and if I head out now, I should get there in an hour or so."

"Okay. Maybe next time," Lincoln said and gave a smile before he shook Sandman's hand. The five men exchanged pleasantries and then Sandman turned toward J.J.

"If you need anything, if you have any questions or concerns that Conway or the others can't assist you with, then Conway will get in touch with me. It would be better to not take any chances communicating with me for a while. Just in case someone caught wind of this operation or whatever," Sandman said as he held J.J.'s gaze. Sandman had a way about him. Even though he was huge and intimidating, he had kindness and empathy in his eyes. Frank had been right. Sandman was definitely trustworthy.

"Okay. As long as these men understand that, too. If I have questions, I expect answers," she added. When she looked at the four men behind Sandman, they seemed to take on a different look. It nearly unnerved her.

Sandman glanced over his shoulder.

"J.J., you're safe here. Conway, Lincoln, Brook, and Calder can and will protect you. They'll answer your questions, and I'm certain they'll have questions of their own," he said. She got his message. They were on a need-to-know basis. She didn't want to talk about what had happened to her and why she was here. God knew if these men held some sort of alliance to Dooley. If they did, she was dead. She wasn't ready to die. Not without a fight, and not before seeing Dooley suffer for his crimes.

* * * *

Lincoln filled the large bowls with stew as Brook sliced the loaf of bread from the local bakery in town. Calder was pouring some sweet tea when J.J. entered the room.

"You can sit over here," Conway stated.

"Can I sit here instead?" she asked, and Conway noticed that it was the seat closest to the entrance to the living room, and where her back was against the wall and she could see around the room. It was his seat. It gave him a funny sensation inside. This woman was on edge and in survival mode.

"Sure thing," he said, and his team looked at him with concern, a bit surprised. He gave a stern expression and they went about getting things ready for dinner.

They ate in silence until Lincoln questioned J.J. on why she wasn't eating.

"Don't you like stew, honey?" he asked her in that special way Lincoln used before to ease the tension, and especially with a woman. Conway nearly laughed when J.J. shot daggers at Lincoln as if she could kick his ass.

"Darlin', we're the good guys, remember? We'd like you to feel comfortable while you're here. If there's something you don't like, then tell us. I can make something different for dinner."

J.J. dropped her fork and stood up.

"I'm not hungry. You don't need to cook for me. I don't need anything. And as far as what I don't like? Questions or bullshit." She stepped away from the table and walked out of the room.

Calder let out a long whistle.

"Wow. You're losing your touch, Lincoln," Calder teased, and then took a bite full of beef stew.

Lincoln stared at the doorway, and then looked at Conway. Conway gave him a somewhat understanding expression. The woman was on the run and hiding. She sure as shit wasn't going to trust them just because Sandman said to. Conway would need more information on her if she kept this up. He lifted his fork and began to eat. He couldn't help but think about the sound of her rumbling stomach earlier. She was hungry, and maybe hadn't eaten right in quite some time.

"Ease up and don't ask her anything. She needs to eat," Conway stated.

"You think she hasn't eaten in a while or something?" Lincoln asked.

"I don't know. I heard her stomach rumble before when we went through the kitchen."

"Fuck," Lincoln said and then ran his fingers through his hair.

"Don't worry about it. We figure this out. We always do," he said and then looked toward the doorway. J.J. was definitely complicated, but there was something about her that piqued his interest. It was in her jade-colored eyes. Despite the fear that he saw there, he noticed something else. Determination, strength, and fire. The woman was fighting, and if he were right, she was fighting for her life.

Chapter 3

The week had passed and it was the same routine. Conway watched her on video surveillance every night, sneaking downstairs to try and eat. She went from eating two forkfuls of food to four. Then she would cover her eyes and lay her head on the table. But it was tonight, right now as he watched her adjust her sweatshirt that he saw the gun she was carrying. He knew she had one under her pillow and a few others around the room. It was their job to know. Conway allowed it, but now, here she was walking around the house armed, and on edge. She could kill one of them. It was time to set some rules.

Conway exited the surveillance room and headed down the hallway. He made his presence known. After all, he didn't want to get his head shot off.

When he walked into the kitchen, J.J. was standing there.

"I didn't mean to wake you up. I was just grabbing a drink of water," she said as she showed him the bottle.

"Why don't you try eating something? You can't live on water," he replied as he held his position in the doorway. He took up the entire space. He was six feet four inches tall and a master at martial arts. So were the others, but he and Lincoln conducted classes at the police academy.

"I'm good," she said.

"No, you're not. Eating two or three forkfuls of food a night won't give you the nutrients you need."

She stared at him and then she figured it out and looked angry.

"Spying on me with your little cameras?"

"It's my job. Just like it is to remind you that we're here to protect you."

"How is that a reminder? Seems more like spying and trying to figure out my weakness."

God, this woman is paranoid. Who made her like this?

"I'm not the kind of guy to mince words, so let's get down to the bottom of this. Hand over the gun, and you can head back to bed."

She stared at him and now stood straighter. He lifted his hand out for her to give him the revolver.

"Since we're getting down to the point, fuck you. It's my gun and it's my right."

Why her denial to his order and the tone of her voice awoke something deep within him, Conway didn't know. But the woman's choice of words, the way she stood feminine and confident in his fucking kitchen, excited him. But he needed to calm her down before the others showed up too. He knew they were probably listening in. None of them had good sleeping habits. They awoke so easily to the smallest sounds.

"Listen, I'm not going to argue about this with you. It's not safe, and it's not necessary to walk around with a gun."

"That's your opinion."

"That's a fact."

"It's your opinion. This is your home, your rules, and your safe location. To me this is unknown territory, you and your team are strangers, and I don't know anything about you or your abilities. Excuse me if I want to secure my own weapon as I walk around, but that's not going to change."

"It will change. You're hotheaded, you're on the edge of a breakdown, and God knows if you even know how to use that thing."

"Oh, I know how to use it. You don't know what I've been through. Lots of people and places have claimed to be safe, and then they're infiltrated. Good night, Conway. My gun stays with me."

She headed toward him, and then stopped when he didn't move.

He stared down into her jade green eyes, and she suddenly uncrossed her arms.

He felt the attraction immediately. It seemed that she felt it too, because suddenly he was moving out of the way and she was sprinting to her room.

Holy shit. Where the hell did that come from?

* * * *

J.J. couldn't sleep. She was tossing and turning, and kept waking up with a jolt or in a sweat. The nightmares were getting worse, and so were the shakes. She even cut off having coffee and other caffeine related drinks. But it wasn't working. Knowing that today was Sunday, she decided to do something to keep her mind off the nightmares and the shaking. She wished she could work out, or go for a run. But that didn't seem feasible. She wanted to ask the guys, but they disappeared during the day, except for one of them. One of them was always around to keep watch. Usually it was Brook.

She walked into the kitchen. It was early, and the guys were up by six. The clock read 5:00 a.m. She pulled out some pans, and took the bacon from the refrigerator. Looking around the cabinets, she found the ingredients she needed to make pancakes and then a container with chocolate chips. She decided to make chocolate chip pancakes and bacon. Although she felt kind of funny doing this and making herself at home in their kitchen, she needed this. She needed to find some kind of normalcy to what was happening.

She didn't know these men. They were huge, they were intimidating, and supposedly retired from the military. When she asked further questions, Sandman stated that it wasn't important for her to know. Hadn't she said the same thing to them about her? Wouldn't she remain silent and not share too much about who she really was and why she was here? She was kept up for too long, and forced to stop everything that would make her feel strong again. She wanted to exercise, to hit a punching bag and release some anger.

Before the first piece of bacon hit the pan, Lincoln entered the kitchen.

"What are you up to?" he asked with an attitude.

"Cooking breakfast. I couldn't sleep."

"I know," he stated and then walked over to the coffeepot and poured himself a cup. She started that, too, as she gathered the ingredients.

She hoped that she hadn't made any sounds. She had slept with the pillow partially over her head in hopes of muffling any sounds she may make during her sleep. It was crazy and a bit uncomfortable considering that she awoke more often than not, feeling Dexter choking her against the car, the pillow blocking her breathing making it worse.

She shivered from the thought, despite the turtleneck she wore, and nearly burnt the bacon.

"Whoa. Hey, let me take care of that," Lincoln said as he slowly took the tongs from her hand, and placed his hand on her waist to guide her out of the way.

She looked up at him.

"I'm sorry," she whispered and turned toward the bowl. She hadn't even realized what she was doing. *Am I losing my mind?*

"J.J.? Are you okay?" Lincoln asked her.

She saw the concern on his face. His blond crew cut hair, the way his shirt clung to tight, large muscles, gave her an odd sensation. His green eyes seemed filled with concern, as well as the hard expression on his chiseled face. The man was very handsome in a rugged, hard, experienced kind of way. He was also older. The tattoos on his forearms, similar to Calder's, gave her the impression that he was hard, and dangerous. But then, he spoke so softly to her. Was it a way to draw her in, and then pounce?

"What's going on?" Conway asked as he entered the room.

"Nothing," she whispered and turned toward the mixing bowl. She needed to focus on the task at hand and not the terrifying thoughts of her undercover operation. She could handle this, just like she'd handled everything else thus far.

"You're up kind of early," Conway said as he poured himself a cup of coffee.

"You are, too," she replied, and they locked gazes.

It was like a game. She wanted to figure out who they really were and whether or not they were trustworthy, and they were doing the same with her. She didn't like feeling as if she were living in a fishbowl. Why did they have to watch her every move? It was unnerving, especially since certain body parts immediately reacted.

"I have some things to go over in the surveillance room with Lincoln. Brook and Calder will be around the house. If you need anything, just holler."

"I won't need anything," she replied and then started to make the pancakes. She had to truly focus on the task at hand to not burn these damn things, too. Why the hell did she decide to take on this task? Especially now, when she felt so out of control of her emotions?

* * * *

Lincoln shot Conway a look as they gathered in the surveillance room after breakfast. J.J. had disappeared once again, after only having half a pancake and part of a strip of bacon. He was a bit concerned about J.J. She had totally been lost in thought and nearly burned the bacon. He'd caught her lose focus before and completely forget what she was doing. Calder mentioned that he'd witnessed her doing the same thing. If they could just get her to open up a little about her situation, maybe they could help her.

"Is it me, or does it seem like after she zones out, she shivers as if she's recalling something that was bad or hurt?" he asked Conway.

"You're probably right. Sandman didn't give us much to go on. His friend, however he knows J.J., was insistent that we get basic information."

"That's bothering me a lot right now, Conway."

"It's the way it is. We know the basics. She's in some kind of danger. Protective custody wasn't an option with the risk of attempt so high. Sandman hinted around about her being pretty damn tough."

"What do you think she was involved in? Mafia related maybe?"

"Not certain, Conway. Maybe she'll come around and give us some info. In the interim, our orders are pretty straightforward. Protect her. Don't let her out of our sight, and don't trust anyone. I'd say the ones who are after her have some resources of their own."

"Fuck," Lincoln replied, not liking the feeling he had inside, and about this situation at all. He wanted to know more. But right now, J.J. was their only source for information and she wasn't budging.

* * * *

Calder came into the kitchen looking for J.J.

He had updated the surveillance cameras and completed the monthly check of the equipment. Everything was operational. He had a hard time focusing on his work as he thought about the woman staying in their home. She was quite stunning, and as he had the opportunity to watch her while she wasn't looking, he found himself concerned over her injury. That hit to her face must have been a good one. She also wore a lot of high-collared shirts or turtlenecks. He wondered if she were hiding more injuries. The thought bothered him. She was very attractive and seemed to have a great body to boot. But she hid it well.

He decided to check on her and see what she liked to do as a hobby. Brook had his workshop out back, where he made his own carved wood furniture. That was the best decision Brook had made in the right step toward recovery. His PTSS had been getting the better of him when he first returned home from the service. They all suffered from the same condition and had to find their own means of coping with it. Brook had his furniture carving, Conway had his professional occupation as chief of police, Lincoln had the martial arts training and cooking, as well as surveillance operations, and Calder did the same. He worked on updating and improving surveillance and monitoring equipment as well as creating undetectable bombs and other means of weaponry. He helped to train police officers in self-defense and hand-to-hand combat. He didn't like cooking and he wasn't a talker. He tended to keep his emotions bottled up and presented his character by action not words.

Conway teased him about the display of intense tattoos on both his arms and his back. He liked his tattoos and they all had meaning. From the American flag to the names of his buddies lost in combat, they were part of his life and the person he was.

He locked up the surveillance room and headed down the hall to check on J.J.

J.J. had said that she wanted to lie down in her bedroom over an hour ago. Being Special Forces for so many years, it was easy for him to move around the house without being detected. Well, at least from J.J., not the others. They were just as highly trained. Calder felt compelled to check on her. She wasn't coming out of her shell or really speaking to any of them. It had been nearly three weeks since she'd arrived, and nothing had changed. If anything, she seemed more distant.

As he approached the doorway, he noticed it was ajar. A quick glance inside and he could see her on the bed, arms holding on to the backboard behind her, as she lifted her thighs all the way up in the air and slowly lowered them, using her abdominal muscles. She only wore a tank top and a pair of baggy, thin sweats. Immediately he noticed the bruises around her neck, her chest, and arms. His chest tightened. Had someone tried to strangle her?

His gaze stretched along the rest of her perfect body. The woman was muscular, as if she worked out on a regular basis. He was impressed. She continued to do the hard abdominal workout, and he felt a bit embarrassed for spying on her. Then he got an idea. Conway wasn't sure why he was even thinking this much about J.J. and her possible situation, but he was. Just as they all had suffered some hard, difficult experiences in their past, it seemed that J.J. had too. What if there was a way to help her open up? This exercise thing was the first indication of who she may be and what type of personality she had. They all enjoyed a good workout. They had the gym.

He walked away, being sure to not make any noise. Then he walked back toward her room, calling her name.

She quickly made it to the doorway.

"Yeah?" she answered, appearing flushed and a bit out of breath.

"What are you doing?" he asked her.

"Nothing."

"You seem winded. Are you exercising?" he asked, and she looked him over and opened the door all the way. She walked around the room and began to look behind the shades, above and behind the mirror.

"Now what are you doing?"

"Looking for cameras. Are you spying on me again?" she asked, sounding annoyed. He couldn't help but chuckle.

Honey, if I wanted to spy on you and place cameras in this room, you'd never be able to find them.

"Of course not. I just put two and two together, ya know?"

"No, I don't know," she said with attitude as she crossed her arms in front of her chest.

"The outfit. The sweat on your brow. Your flushed complexion. Unless I'm wrong, and I made you blush and perspire."

"As if," she retorted. He laughed again.

He stared at the bruising and could see the finger marks. *Son of a bitch. Someone definitely had their hands around her neck tight enough to cause that kind of bruising.*

He must have been staring too long because she reached up and placed her hand over her neck.

"Do those hurt?" he asked, tilting his head toward her, his eyes still on her neck. He also absorbed the fullness of her breasts and the deep cleavage between them. He was human, and he was a man. J.J. had a body like some sex symbol.

"I'm fine."

"So you keep saying."

"Well, I am."

"Sure you are."

"I am," she stated with her teeth clenched, and she took a step toward him. He raised one eyebrow at her. The woman was on the brink. She was ready to explode with anger. Where was all the aggression coming from?

"Listen, if you want to work out, you could have asked if we had a gym."

She uncrossed her arms.

"You have a gym?" she asked, stepping toward him.

Ahhh, so she likes to work out? Now I'm making some progress.

"Sure we have a gym. Lincoln and I do martial arts training. Brook and Conway are really good, too. We have a combination dojo and regular gym out back in the huge barn."

"Why didn't you mention this earlier?"

"You didn't ask."

"I didn't know that you were into martial arts. I mean, you guys are all in great physical condition."

"You think so, huh?" he asked as he gave her a flirty look. He hadn't even thought before he did it. It just happened, and now he felt like an idiot. This wasn't him. Calder Murphy did not flirt.

"Come on, Calder. Tell me what else you have hidden on this ranch. I need something more to do than just sit around here and think. I feel like I'm losing my mind."

"Thinking is good."

"Not from where my mind wanders to. I need a gym. I love working out and doing physical activities. Could I use the gym? I mean, if you and the team didn't mind, of course."

"You can use it, but one of us has to be with you."

She shook her head. "That's lame."

"Those are the rules. The gym and dojo are out back. We're here to protect you, even though we have no idea from who or what," he said and then uncrossed his arms. She just stared at him.

"Come on. I'll show it to you now. But bring a sweatshirt. It's getting chilly out there."

They headed outside together. Calder opened the door and there was Lincoln, working out on the bags. A quick glance at J.J. and she was trying her hardest not to stare at Lincoln but instead take in the dojo and the gym.

Lincoln grabbed the black bag he was kicking and turned to look at them.

"Hey, what's going on? Is everything all right?" he asked filled with concern.

Calder nodded.

"Everything is good. I was talking to J.J. and told her about the gym. She likes to work out, so I thought we could show her the equipment and what we have."

"Sounds good, but you can't come out here alone. One of us has to be with you," Lincoln stated very seriously.

"All of you are right inside. Don't you have this place all wired up with cameras and other things anyway?" she asked with an attitude.

"Those are the rules. You don't like it? Tough," Calder stated, with his arms crossed in front of his chest.

She stared up at him. Now, being this close to her, he absorbed the scent of her perfume, the deep jade color of her eyes, and the thick eyelashes that blinked as she rolled her eyes at him. He had to hide his chuckle. It seemed J.J. wasn't used to being ordered around.

"He's right. So, what do you like to do? We have ellipticals, treadmills, free weights, mats for yoga, and we can get videos if you like aerobics or something like that?" Lincoln asked.

She walked deeper into the room and ran her hand along the boxing bags, the sets of gloves, and other martial arts equipment. Then she looked at the dojo, where the large padded floor sat, with other training devices for martial arts.

"I can use what you have here."

"Do you have any training in martial arts?" Lincoln asked. She looked up toward him.

"Some," she said and then walked around the room. She looked at the pictures on the wall. Some were of the team with the training academy. Some were from when they were in the service.

"All four of you were in the military?" she asked.

"Yes," Calder said as he walked deeper into the room.

She leaned forward and squinted her eyes at one picture in the top right corner. They were in uniform with the entire team, but she wouldn't know what the symbol stood for. It was an elite group of soldiers. Special Forces and then some.

"Special Forces, huh? Impressive."

Calder looked at Lincoln.

"What do you know about it?" Lincoln asked on the defensive. He was always on guard when it came to their pasts and their service history.

She locked gazes with him. "Enough," she said, and Calder wondered if she knew someone in that troop. Half of them were dead. Killed in action or lost somewhere.

"Well, I didn't mean to interrupt your workout, Lincoln. If you don't mind, I'll just mess around a little, and check the place out."

"Fine with me. Calder, you want to spar?" Lincoln asked.

"Sure," Calder stated as he pulled his hooded sweatshirt up and over his head. He caught J.J. staring, and shockingly, he liked it.

* * * *

J.J. couldn't believe how attracted she was to these men. She realized pretty quickly that there was something about each of them that pulled at her feminine strings. Calder's tough attitude, the tattoos on his arms, the intensity in his dark gray eyes, and the way he seemed to notice every little thing on her. Then, of course, Lincoln. Blond hair, crew cut, green eyes, six feet three, the man was very attractive. Add in the fact that he could cook and also trained martial arts, and she was instantly attracted. Brook was the most unique one of the four. He was quiet, brooding, and seemed empathetic and caring. If that was even right to describe a retired Special Forces guy as caring and quiet. His deep brown eyes were soothing. Whenever she caught him watching her, it was like he could see into her soul. But it wasn't unnerving, it seemed like he got it. He understood her need to be on the defensive. But then there was Conway. The man didn't say much. He appeared to be in charge all of the time, or perhaps his team just let him be. He took his position as chief of police very seriously. The sight of him in uniform reminded her so much of Anthony, but the fact that they were all trained, and trained others in martial arts and were Special Forces, really was the kicker.

That was Anthony. Her trainer, her instructor in the special investigative unit, and he was a black belt in Tae Kwon Do. He spent years in the military prior to entering the police department, and she knew he was part of a Special Forces team. She couldn't help but wonder if the men had known Anthony.

She shook her head. That would be so crazy.

She needed to clear her mind. If she could just get past the images that flooded her brain and were triggered by the stupidest things, then maybe she could let her guard down a tad. But then again, what if these men weren't as good as Frank thought, or what if they could be paid off? Then they would know more about her and ways to destroy her or ultimately kill her. She couldn't do that.

Instantly she felt her body tense.

"Hey. Are you okay?" Lincoln placed his hand on her shoulder and she twisted to the right and slammed his hand down. She was in a ready stance, prepared to fight.

"Whoa. It's okay, J.J.," he said.

"You zoned out, again," Calder added and he looked concerned.

"I'm fine. I just need to work out. Can I jump in with you guys? Sparring, I mean?"

"I don't know if you should. You could get hurt," Lincoln said and she gave him a jab in his stomach. Not too hard, but not too light either.

He shook his head, as Calder gave her a stern expression.

"You don't know what you're getting yourself into, darling," he said and she walked to the left and took a shot at him. Calder dodged it.

"I think I'll be the one to decide that." And so it began.

Calder and Lincoln took turns sparring with J.J. They moved in a circular rotation and she countered most of what they threw at her. They were giving her a nice workout, but they were playing with her and taking it easy. She didn't want easy. She wanted to rid her mind of the memories, the horrific thoughts and fears plaguing her brain. She was lost in her thoughts now, even as they sparred. It was like she was having an out-of-body experience, or her mind was divided into two parts. The one that followed the movements of her body as she sparred with Lincoln and Calder, and the part that recalled the events that led to her being here, on the run, living with danger breathing down her back.

Calder nearly swept her feet out from under her but she recovered and jabbed him in the side. It must have been kind of hard because he paused to look at her a moment, and then there she was again. Her mind flashed to Dexter. He was choking her. Trying to take the life from her. She remembered thinking that she was going to die, and that Dooley was going to get away with murder, killing Tara, Marlee, and Denise.

She realized that she was getting too rough. She was trying to take out her anger and aggression on Calder and Lincoln. She yanked off her sweatshirt and turned toward the long black bag. She started hitting it, punching it, kicking it. She was running on all the anger and energy she had kept up in her. The flashbacks, the pain, the fear, as she kicked that bag, lifted her thigh higher, and imagined that it was Dexter, and she was defending herself. She was going to town on it until she couldn't go any further, and then she fell to the mat onto her knees and slammed her palms on the black padding.

She was breathing heavy, and she felt the two men behind her. Lincoln and Calder.

She looked up toward them. Calder was staring at her. Lincoln's eyes were transfixed on her neck, and probably the bruising on her body. It looked ugly and dark. She took a deep breath and released it.

"God, I needed that. I needed to just get that out," she said.

Lincoln squatted down next to her. He reached out and placed his fingers under her chin. He turned her face gently.

"Those look terrible. I have some cream that can help take the bruising away quicker." His eyes darted to her cheekbone and the bruise there, and then to her eyes.

"Want to tell us how you got these?"

"You're already in enough danger, just being around me," she said and turned her face.

"Explain," Calder said in a stern voice. She looked at him and his bulging muscles. At six feet four, the man was huge compared to her and especially now as he stood up straight and she was kneeling on the mat.

Slowly she started to get up. Lincoln jumped up, and then reached down to assist her. When he touched her elbow and placed a hand on her waist, she turned toward him. Her body was shaking and she felt exhausted. She was, both physically and emotionally.

"I think I overdid it," she said, feeling her head spin. She prayed that she wouldn't faint.

"Avoiding the order is not going to let it disappear," Calder stated.

"Order?" she asked as Lincoln released her. He walked to the side and grabbed her a bottle of water.

"Here, drink this." She took it from him with shaking hands and opened up the cap. She drank it, as her eyes looked at Calder over the edge of the bottle.

His arms were crossed in front of his chest and he looked like a muscle man.

"First of all, I don't take orders from you, Calder. Secondly, I don't need to share shit with you, unless I want to."

His eyebrow lifted in surprise and challenge. She felt her gut clench.

"You don't think you have to take orders from me?" he asked, stepping toward her.

She stepped toward him. "No. I don't. You think I'm scared of you?" she asked, and then looked over his muscles, and then back up into his eyes. Those tattoos were definitely intimidating.

"You should watch your attitude around here. We don't tolerate it."

"Oh, really? What are you going to do about it?" she asked and stepped closer. Now they were toe to toe and she was staring up into his eyes and slightly over his huge chest.

"There's ways of dealing with recalcitrant behavior," Lincoln added, and when she looked toward him, surprised that he was adding to this, Calder made his move.

She froze the second his palm cupped her cheek and his other hand gripped her hip. He was staring down into her eyes, her chest was moving up and down slowly, and she realized that her breasts looked huge in the tank top. He held her gaze.

"When are you going to stop fighting us and let us help you?"

She thought about that a moment. They seemed like good men, trustworthy men, but how could she be sure? She couldn't.

"I can't," she whispered, hearing the defeat in her tone. Then she felt the hand on her shoulder from behind. It was Lincoln.

"You can. The more we know, the better we can protect you."

"I can't. I'm sorry, but it's not a risk I'm willing to take. Not now. Not after the first protection operation nearly killed me. I'm sorry," she said and then tried to pull away. Neither man allowed it. Calder stared at her.

"You were in protective custody and the team in charge failed you?" he asked. She swallowed hard. The stupid feds thought that two agents and a peephole in the hotel were enough to secure her until evidence was gathered and a case made.

"They were stupid. They underestimated the criminal."

"What happened to the ones who were supposed to protect you?" Calder asked.

"They died," she whispered, remembering the two agents who'd totally backcrossed the FBI. They were working for Dooley. The congressman had people everywhere. Could he even somehow get to these men?

"How did you survive? How did you get out of there?" Lincoln asked.

"The criminals underestimated the victim," she said.

"Did the ones protecting you help to get you out alive before they were killed?" Calder asked. She chuckled softly.

"They were paid off by the criminal. I was as good as dead." She lowered her eyes, recalling the feelings of defeat and distrust. Could she ever trust another person fully again? Was she even capable of it after all of this?

Calder ran his thumb back and forth over her skin as he held her face.

"We're not going to let anything happen to you. The more we know, the better we can protect you."

She shook her head.

"It's only a matter of time. It's not if, it's when they come. I will be ready. I'm not going to die without a fight. I have nothing else to live for, but to see justice served."

Chapter 4

"What the hell do you mean you have no idea where the hell she went? She's a fucking woman. How could she escape your grasp and simply disappear? I've got dead bodies to hide, and another two fucking federal agents to add to the list of murders we're connected to. I want that bitch dead," Congressman Dooley yelled into the phone.

He was at his wit's end. Somehow that undercover investigator had gotten away and right after he admitted to murdering other women. He should have grabbed that whore by her neck, did her like he did Tara, and then slit her fucking throat. One stinking bitch was not going to destroy his life, his family, and everything he'd worked so damn hard for.

"You know we're trying, sir. There's a lot to cover up. Too many loose ends, and too many witnesses at the casino, never mind the hotel where we were supposed to snag her. The woman is tough and she's resourceful," his head of security stated.

"Well, tell me something I don't know. She's smarter than you? Smarter than the team of government agents that are to protect my name, cover my ass, and let me get away with anything I want?"

"This situation has gotten out of control. Perhaps leaving her alone, and letting her think that you've given up will help us to catch her."

"In the interim, I've got spies trying to infiltrate my company, the secret agents investigating my activities both on paper and in Nevada for the last ten years, and my reelection is in jeopardy. My wife isn't talking to me. Reporters are trying to do their own investigations into my connection to the Vegas murders, while you and the rest of my team are trying to cut loose strings? I've got the local Nevada State Police applying pressure and asking questions and I don't like the direction they're going in. They're going back in their records. They're looking at the fuck up drug operation in the warehouse from two years ago. What the fuck? You need to handle this. Some fucking bitch is not taking me down. Make it go away. Find her, eliminate the problem and anyone else who may be helping her, and let's wrap this up."

He hung up the phone and stared out the window. "How the fuck did this get so bad, so quickly?"

His phone rang again. This time from his private disposable cell phone. It was how he handled all his illegal business connections. Glancing at the number, he knew that it was Martin McCue.

"Got any good news for me?"

"No. She's gone under the radar. I've got people on the inside of the Nevada State Police. We've been trailing her commander, Frank Reynolds, and we've tapped his office lines as well as his home lines. All we came up with thus far is a call to an unsolicited number out in Texas. My resources can't penetrate this number, however, yours may be able to."

The congressman thought about it a moment. He was willing to do anything to wipe this shit from his life.

"Give me the number and I'll get the info to you ASAP."

"Great. Hopefully this will lead to finding her. I'd like to personally take care of this for you, Congressman. I don't want our business to be over, and it would bring me great pleasure to torture that bitch."

"She's all yours. Just be sure to get rid of her. She's nothing but a worthless cop, and I'm a fucking congressman. Does she really think she can take me down? Not happening."

He disconnected the call and quickly looked up the number of someone he believed he could trust. Delaney something. He picked up the phone again and dialed her number.

Midconversation, as he heard her typing away on the government computer, she paused.

"Sir, were you ever able to find out anything with my sister's case? You said that you'd check into it?"

Dooley cringed. He hated when people asked him for favors. He couldn't even remember Delaney's last name, never mind any conversation about her sister. What the fuck was she talking about?

"I'm sorry, but there was nothing I could do."

"How can that be? I thought you were personal friends with the CEO of that company."

"Listen, Delaney, I'm on a tight schedule today. Do me a favor, get me the info I need right now, and then send the info about your sister to my secretary. I'll look over the problem again and see what I can do, okay?" he stated with an attitude and he got no response. Instead he heard the tapping of keys and then Delaney's monotone voice.

"That number is a secure line coming from the Nevada State Police to a private secure line in Houston, Texas. Give me a moment and I will have a name and address."

Dooley smiled. Whoever was helping her was about to go down, big time.

* * * *

It had been two days since the incident in the gym with Calder, Lincoln, and J.J. Lincoln remained toward the back of the room as J.J. ran on the elliptical and then started hitting the punching bag. He saw her pause a moment and lay her forehead against the bag. He was filled with concern for her. Why couldn't she just trust them?

She seemed like she was getting a bit more comfortable with them. That was a plus. She'd actually eaten dinner with them last night and breakfast this morning. Her appetite was getting better. Maybe the working out was helping.

Lincoln was stretching out on the mats after his workout, when he sensed J.J. approaching.

She sat down on the mat across from him and began stretching.

"What's up with all the tattoos? You like pain or something?" she asked, in that abrupt tone they were getting used to but to him didn't seem like J.J.'s style. She was just on edge and trying to act tough. If she would just give a little, and let them know she was willing to accept their sincerity, then maybe they could get to know her better.

"I like them. They all have meaning," he said.

She looked at his forearms as she stretched her hand down to her toes on one side. The move gave him a great view of her breasts in the tank top she wore.

"I get the American flag and the wicked Special Forces symbol, but what's with the names and the dark images? You and Calder both have them."

He looked down at his left arm first.

"These are some of my buddies who died in combat." He looked at his other arm.

"Same here. I guess it's my way of honoring them and never forgetting their sacrifices."

"That's cool. What were some of the names?" she asked and tried to look. He wondered why she was asking. He had this funny feeling in his gut. It was like she thought she might know them. Had she known one of his team members? But how? What was the likelihood?

"You won't know any of them."

She started to say something and then stopped. She stretched out her other leg while tucking the first leg she'd stretched up and against her belly.

"Did they all die in combat or did any of them make it back to civilian life?" she asked.

"These guys died in battle alongside us."

"You mean you were in combat with them when they died?"

"Yeah. We were all involved in some very heavy shit."

She stared at him, and he felt like they were making some sort of a connection. But he was still on guard. J.J. was so unpredictable.

"Was it hard for you? For Calder, Brook, and Conway to adapt back to being civilians, after experiencing the things you experienced?" she asked.

He thought about her question. Perhaps she was reaching out for information and this could be a way for him to help her.

"Well, you probably heard about post-traumatic stress syndrome? We all suffered from it when we returned."

"How did you gain control of it?"

"Well, we still suffer from it really. Our daily activities help us. We've trained our minds to not give so much power to the thoughts, the memories of the bad times."

"How do you do that? I mean, doesn't it feel like your mind has more control than you do?"

He took a deep breath and released a soft sigh. This was making progress.

"J.J., PTSS can be very serious if it isn't treated. Or at minimum, not shared with people who care. As I mentioned earlier, we all suffered from it. We don't sleep well at night. We always keep an eye on what's going on around us, and having this place fully wired with surveillance helps us to ensure our minds that the enemy isn't going to infiltrate the perimeter of our property and home."

She looked around the room and then leaned back on the palms of her hands.

"Then you're lucky that you have one another."

"Hey, I'm here for you, and you're not alone in this."

She shot him a look.

"We were talking about you. Not me," she snapped.

"Were we now?"

"Yeah, we were. I don't have that PTSS, and I'm all alone in this world. I don't have my military buddies, or the capabilities to wire anything to ensure my safety. I don't even have a home anymore because the fucker blew it up." She stood up and so did Lincoln.

"The person who you're hiding from blew up your fucking home?" he asked.

She closed her eyes and took a deep breath. She was trying to calm herself down.

"Listen, Lincoln, I don't know why you guys are doing this. I don't know why Sandman recommended the four of you, and I don't know what the outcome of all this will be. I've pretty much accepted my fate. I'm going to die. They are going to find me and erase everything that happened and no one is going to give a fuck. So please, don't patronize me and tell me that you're here for me, when you don't even know me."

"You don't know us or our capabilities. If you just let us in on this, we can better understand the situation. You're not alone anymore. If you just start showing us some trust, and some sort of commitment to this situation and let us in, then we can and will protect you fully, with our lives. You don't ever have to be alone again, J.J. Show us that you trust us."

She started to walk backward. He could see the tears in her eyes, the struggle in her gaze as she shook her head.

"I don't know how to. I'm sorry," she whispered and then headed out of the room.

He grabbed his sweatshirt and followed her, but not before glancing at the camera, knowing that someone from his team was watching and listening.

* * * *

Calder and Brook were in the surveillance room.

"I'd call that progress, but damn, is she fucking scared. I want to know who hurt her. I want to know who put that fear in her eyes and what happened that she's suffering from PTSS. Lincoln is right. We can help her," Brook stated.

The soft beeping sound indicated that someone was approaching the roadway leading up to the property by motor vehicle. A quick glance toward the cameras by the front gate and they spotted the small red sports car.

"Pauline. Damn, why can't that woman leave us alone?"

"Because she's obsessed with winning Conway and your attention," Brook stated.

"She's a pain in the ass, and we need to get her out of here before she sees J.J.," Calder said.

"I'm on it. Be careful about insulting her again, or she'll complain to Conway, and start harassing him again too. It's my fault anyway. I was in a bad state that night. Between the Jack Daniels and the flashbacks, I was on the way to destruction."

"Yeah, that little lady was on her way to landing an orgy none of us were interested in."

* * * *

J.J. could hear what Brook and Calder were saying as she stood by the door. Calder walked out and gave her a look. "Stay here, and don't move. Don't go by any windows or anything."

He was so damn forceful, and she gave him a dirty look. Of course Calder pointed at her, daring her to challenge him. Instead she turned away and saw the surveillance room. There were about eight different small flat screens, a whole lot of special equipment, and Brook. He was staring at one screen and moving a flat mouse pad around on his desk as the picture enlarged.

J.J. saw the blonde, and instantly she had an odd feeling in her gut. Then she saw Calder walking outside, and Lincoln making his way over from the barn. Both men looked annoyed, but Calder appeared pissed off. "Fuck, Calder, just let Lincoln get rid of her," Brook whispered.

"Who's the blonde? Old girlfriend of Calder's?" J.J. asked as she walked further into the room. Brook never let his eyes off the screen. She hadn't snuck up on him. The man knew she was there the whole time.

"No. She's just interested and we're not."

J.J. wondered what Brook meant by "we're" and whether the blonde was after all four of them.

"Who is she?" J.J. asked.

"A local girl, set on landing a few men of her own." Brook turned toward J.J. as Calder spoke to the woman and Lincoln kept his arms crossed in front of his chest.

J.J. walked closer and stared at Calder and Lincoln. They were really annoyed at this woman, and she seemed oblivious as she headed toward the house.

"What do you mean, land a few men?" she asked as she stood by the desk and looked at the other cameras.

"A ménage."

J.J. took her eyes off the screen and stared at Brook. He was facing her, still sitting in the chair, and looking awfully serious. For some odd reason, her pussy seemed to react to the word ménage.

She swallowed hard.

"Are you serious? She wants Calder and Lincoln?" she asked, her voice actually cracking as she turned to look at the screen and saw the blonde heading toward the house and the back kitchen door. Both Calder and Lincoln were on her heels trying to stop her. The blonde wrapped herself around Calder and started kissing his neck and climbing his body.

"And me and Conway, too. It's a common type of relationship around these parts. It takes a special connection though, for it to work out," Brook whispered.

For some strange reason, J.J. felt her nipples harden and her reply catch in her throat.

She had heard about such relationships before, and had seen some crazy shit in Vegas. But the way Brook spoke of this type of relationship, he seemed interested.

"So she wants the four of you?" J.J. asked, and when she turned toward him, he was staring at her neck.

He reached for her chin. "Is this why you were wearing the turtlenecks? You were hiding these from us?"

She stared up into his eyes. Brook seemed completely upset. His expression was so unnerving.

"You don't need to be afraid of us. You can ask me anything that you want to."

A series of crazy thoughts went through her mind. She could ask him lots of things and learn all about him, Conway, Calder, and Lincoln. But then what would happen when danger found her? She would feel guilty for getting them killed, for getting close to them, or even simply becoming their friend. She couldn't do that. She couldn't risk having friends, opening up her heart to emotions that would only weaken her and expose her to pain. After Anthony died, a part of her died, too. But Lincoln's words came back to her. He wanted her to show them a sign that she could let them in, and trust them. Could she? Were they men she could trust her life with? The thought freaked her out. How could she show them? What if she was wrong? Dead wrong?

"I don't have any questions, Brook. It's better this way."

He squinted his eyes at her.

"Better, why? Are you planning on leaving here? Do you not realize that we're in this for the long haul? What happened in your life, aside from whatever it is we're protecting you from, to make you so fearful to connect?"

Her eyes widened at his interpretation. Brook nailed it on the head. But before she could respond, they heard Calder raising his voice and telling someone to get out.

"I think your friend needs some help."

He looked reluctant to release his hold on her chin. And as crazy as it was, she felt the loss of his touch immediately when he stepped away. She looked at the screen on the wall as she took a deep breath. The woman sat at the kitchen table holding J.J.'s sweatshirt. She was staring at the three men with daggers in her eyes, and Calder looked about ready to lose it.

J.J. stepped out of the surveillance room. She could hear the woman's voice. "Who is she?" she asked.

"There isn't anyone. We're not interested in you. We've told you that before. Now please leave. We're in the middle of something," Lincoln stated, and by his tone, J.J. could tell that he was frustrated. Then she heard the door open and Conway's stern voice.

"What in God's name is she doing here?"

"She wouldn't leave. She showed up and forced her way into the house," Calder said.

"How the hell can she force herself in here?" Conway asked.

"Oh, Calder, come on now, honey. That's not how it went down. You were all over me outside. You practically carried me in here," the woman said. J.J. couldn't believe it. The woman was lying. It really pissed her off that she was doing this, but what could J.J. do?

The bickering continued, and J.J. realized that these four very strong-minded, yet rational men really couldn't physically throw the woman out of their home, but she wasn't getting the message that they didn't want her. Feeling annoyed at hearing the continued back and forth banter, J.J. took matters into her own hands.

She pulled off her jeans and tossed them behind the couch. Then she lifted off the T-shirt and pulled the white guinea tee down as far as it could go, which barely covered her panties or her ass. She looked in the mirror on the wall, saw her boobs pouring from the tank top, and undid the ponytail in her hair and let her long brown locks hang down. She ran her hands through the strands of hair and then shook her head, making her appear well loved or in this case well fucked by at least three of the four men. She licked her lips and then stood in the living room near the couch, where she tossed one of the bottom cushions onto the floor, as if she'd had a wild time with the men.

She could hear the woman arguing with Calder, as Calder sounded like he was telling the woman to back off.

"Calder! Calder, when are you coming back? I need you," J.J. called out.

She stood in her most sexy, yet innocent-looking pose, with her hands pressing the tank down further, and her ass sticking slightly out to the side, as the woman ran into the room.

The blonde gasped as Calder, Lincoln, Brook, and Conway followed her inside. J.J. tried her hardest to ignore the expressions of hunger and obvious excitement in seeing her practically naked in their living room. J.J. knew she had a voluptuous figure, but it had been years since she'd done anything so bold. Anthony had been her one and only lover.

"Who the hell is she?" the blonde asked.

"Calder? What's going on? Brook said that you were going to be here to give me a massage, and then you all disappeared and I heard yelling."

J.J. ignored Conway's angry stare. If her gut was right, he was going to reprimand her for this. Oh well, too late to turn back now.

"You're with her? The four of you are—"

"We've been together for over a month. Who the hell are you?" J.J. asked.

"Honey, I'm theirs. I found them first."

"That's not true, Pauline," Calder began to say.

Pauline shot daggers at J.J., but J.J. knew she was already winning this situation.

J.J. looked the woman over.

"I suggest you get your boney little ass out of my men's house and fast. You better forget their address, their cell numbers, and never come back here again. If you do, I'll personally kick you out. They're being gentlemen, but when it comes to my men, I'm the jealous, crazy type," J.J. said and then stomped her foot forward toward Pauline. Pauline screamed and then went running from the living room. They heard the door slam, and then Brook took a peek into the surveillance room.

"She's gone. She's already heading down the road," he said.

J.J. stared at the four men before her. She didn't know whose expression was more intense. Conway looked downright pissed off. Brook appeared stunned, or just in a daze as he crossed his arms in front of his chest and stared at her. Lincoln was biting his lower lip. As she started to turn to grab her jeans from behind the couch, Calder's voice stopped her.

"Not so fast."

She turned around in time to see him stalking toward her.

"Didn't I tell you to stay put in the surveillance room? Did I not say to stay away from windows?" he asked, and she stepped back. He was intimidating to say the least, but just because she was standing here in the middle of their living room, half-naked, didn't make her some weak female. J.J. placed her hands on her hips and lifted her chin toward Calder.

"I would have, but you apparently didn't have it in you to toss that woman out of your own place. It was annoying to listen to her whine and carry on. Now at least she'll think twice about bothering you again." J.J. turned around and grabbed her pants from the floor. As she stepped into them, the four men watched.

"You think I couldn't toss her out on her ass? I wanted to, but I don't manhandle women. She's young and impressionable. We're older and to her seem adventurous."

"Adventurous, huh? Yeah, Brook told me about Pauline's endeavors with the four of you. Pretty interesting the way y'all do relationships out here in the middle of nowhere." She zipped up her pants and then buttoned the button, putting on a little bit of a Southern accent just to be a wiseass.

"You shouldn't have exposed yourself to her. Now she'll go blabbing around town about you," Conway added to the conversation.

"Listen, it sounded like you needed a woman to get rid of another woman. It's a done deal. You can go back into town and tell all that your latest orgy girl left town. Then you can deal with that Pauline on your own."

"Personally, I think J.J. did us a huge favor. Now Pauline will leave us alone, and no one in town listens to her talk anyway. How many times have you been warned, Conway, that Pauline was after us?" Brook asked, as he stepped forward.

"I agree with Brook. I think J.J. just helped us out. Besides, it's a win-win situation," Lincoln added.

"How is that so?" Calder asked, still sounding pissed off.

"Well, we got Pauline off our case. That's amazing, and we got to see a side of J.J. I personally wouldn't mind seeing some more of," Lincoln stated as he eyed J.J.'s body over.

J.J. chuckled.

"Let's get supper ready. I think that's enough excitement for the evening," Brook stated and then he and Lincoln headed toward the kitchen, but not before winking at J.J. She had to smile.

She was looking for the shirt she'd worn over the tank top when she heard Conway clear his throat. Turning toward him, there he stood beside Calder, and neither man was smiling like Brook and Lincoln just were.

Calder was holding her shirt.

"I didn't need you to get into my business," Calder stated firmly.

She raised one eyebrow at him, as she crossed her arms in front of her chest.

"I thought otherwise."

He stepped closer.

"I don't know where you come from, or what type of job you've had or even the kind of person you are, but in this house, we're in charge. We're here to protect you."

"Okay already, I got it. Now can I have my shirt, please?" She reached her hand out, and he stared at her.

"We got rules around here."

"Okay, Calder, I'll take care of this," Conway said as Calder handed her the shirt and then looked her over before he walked from the room. Now Conway stood there and he was in uniform, leaning his hand on the holster on his hip, and looking too sexy. She had to give herself a mental shake. They were every woman's type.

Conway stared at her, and then stepped closer. He pointed his finger down at her, and she had no place to look but at his face, and the intensity of his eyes, as he towered over her.

"Next time you even remotely disobey an order or place yourself in danger, I'm personally going to throw you over my knee and spank that ass of yours."

J.J. felt her jaw drop, and then saw Conway swallow hard.

"I'd like to see you try that, Chief!"

They stared at one another, and instantly something changed between them. J.J. understood what it was, but suddenly thoughts of the danger that she was in and what could possibly come to these four men hit her hard. She turned away.

"We'll talk more later."

"No need to. I'm sorry if I stepped out of line involving myself in your personal sex life. It won't happen again." She started to head out of the room.

"It won't happen again, and not everyone in this house had sex with Pauline."

She looked him over.

"Good to know, Chief."

She walked away.

* * * *

"What are we going to do about her?" Brook asked Lincoln and Calder. Conway was on the phone in the surveillance room with Sandman.

"Nothing to do. She's got guts, I'll tell you that much," Lincoln said.

"She shouldn't have made her presence known. Pauline could go carrying on at the bar in town about J.J. Then what?" Calder asked.

"It won't matter. Everyone will know that Pauline's pissed that we're taken. J.J.'s move probably helped us finally get Pauline off our asses," Lincoln said.

They were quiet a moment and then Lincoln chuckled.

"What?" Brook asked.

"Calder's face, when he heard J.J.'s voice calling his name."

"What?" Calder asked.

"We were all shocked to hear her. But hot damn, when we entered that living room following Pauline, I thought my heart stopped beating," Lincoln said.

"You? Shit, I think we all know how our bodies reacted to seeing J.J. like that. Damn, that woman has got an amazing body," Brook stated.

"She also has a lot of bruises. Remember, we don't know shit about her, or the situation she's in. How do we know that she didn't cause something? How do we know this doesn't involve drugs, or like you said earlier, mafia shit? She could be one of the bad guys, a seductress, or some thug's lover who was a witness to murder.

Something that the feds are willing to protect her like this," Calder stated. He was pissed off and obviously untrusting.

"You don't know that, Calder. Do you seriously think that she was involved with some criminal, and is a witness to operations or even murder?" Brook asked.

"It could be why the other teams weren't successful in protecting her. Big-time drug lords and gangsters have connections everywhere. In government, in law enforcement departments, and anywhere else they deem fit to be able to destroy people standing in the way of progress and making money," Calder said.

Then they heard voices coming from the living room again and knew it was J.J. and Calder.

* * * *

"We need to talk, J.J. I got some news from Sandman."

She turned back to face him.

"Well?" She felt fearful instantly. Was it already too late? Did Dooley find her? She felt herself begin to teeter, when Conway grabbed on to her and steadied her by her shoulders. She looked at him, feeling instantly helpless now too. For that short period of time, even in angering Conway and Calder, she had forgotten about her situation and the worry.

"It's going to be okay, but I need more information. Someone was able to find out that a commander in the Nevada State Police contacted Sandman out here. A tip from someone inside the federal government, which means they're involved in whatever situation this is, gave the heads-up to a friend of Sandman's."

"Is Frank okay? Please tell me that they didn't go after Frank?" she asked.

* * * *

Conway wasn't sure why he was feeling so out of control right now. The sight of J.J. standing in the living room half-naked with a body of a fucking porn star might have done it. Then, of course, Sandman's update on the abilities these people who were after J.J. had made him feel more protective. But now, hearing her ask about some guy named Frank made him feel jealous. Why the fuck for? She wasn't his or his team's. Although, by the way this scene had gone down tonight, a team meeting and discussion was needed. But first, Conway wanted answers.

"I don't know who Frank is. I'm assuming that he's fine because Sandman didn't indicate otherwise. We've got a lot of friends and connections in the government. We could find out—"

She shook her head. "No. No asking questions or contacting anyone in the government. No. You don't understand. The government can't be trusted. Your police department can't be trusted. These men have so many connections and contacts, the authorities will never be able to find them all. This is bad. They'll kill Frank."

"Who's Frank?" Calder asked as he reentered the room. One look up and Conway knew that his men were there, and they heard the conversation.

J.J. looked at them and then at Conway.

"Who is Frank?" Lincoln asked.

"He's a good friend," she replied as she looked away.

"A good friend or a lover?" Calder asked.

She shot a look at him.

"That's none of your business."

"It is our business if you're going to be focusing on some guy, instead of letting us in on what's going on. Our lives are in jeopardy, too," Calder stated.

"I know that. Don't you think I know that?" she asked, raising her voice.

"Then who the fuck is Frank?" Brook asked this time.

Conway could feel the tension in the room. They were feeling an attraction to J.J. and she was feeling it, too. But he had to remind his men that she was a victim. She wasn't a trained professional like they were. She was more than likely some civilian who had gotten caught in the middle of something crazy. But she wasn't like them.

"Is this Frank guy some drug dealer you were fucking, and then you were picked up by the feds and rolled over to save your ass?" Calder asked.

Conway saw J.J. squint her eyes at Calder and place her hands on her hips. She had changed her clothes. She was wearing a cream-colored blouse with a white camisole underneath it and blue jeans. She wore no shoes on her feet, and Calder was a few feet in front of her, towering over J.J.

"What the fuck are you talking about?" She raised her voice at Calder. He stepped closer.

"You. Who the fuck are you? Why are you here, who is after you, and who the fuck is Frank?"

"Don't you think it's better if you don't know? Don't you understand the danger you'll be placed in if you know all the details?" she asked.

"Fuck, no, lady. We're trained men. We were Special fucking Forces, not some academy trained federal agents. We've seen and done shit that would make your pretty little stomach lose its lunch," Calder stated angrily. J.J. stood her ground.

"I've seen my share of shit, too. The less you know, the better."

"That isn't going to work, J.J.," Conway stated.

"I'm telling you, Conway, she's a fucking criminal. We're protecting her, keeping her under wraps and in hiding until a trial or some shit."

"You are so far off, Calder. For some fucking Special Forces guy, you sure can't figure out shit," J.J. said, and Conway realized that this was getting way out of hand. Both Calder and J.J. seemed to be stubborn individuals, and despite Calder's larger, intimidating appearance, J.J. wasn't backing down.

"Oh, really? I can't figure out who you are? Let's see, you know some self-defense moves. Most women who are smart should know some, but you enjoy boxing more. You probably learned it on the streets, or in the local shitty neighborhood you grew up in. You have an attitude and a mouth on you, always trying to prove that you're tough and can handle everything on your own. That probably means you've had a tough life. Who the fuck hasn't?" he stated angrily and then Lincoln joined in.

"You carry a gun and have multiple others in your room, so you're familiar with weapons and how to use them. Could be family background or survival techniques."

"You thought nothing of playing that role earlier to get rid of Pauline. You're used to pretending to be someone you're not or you're used to using your body to get what you want," Lincoln added.

J.J. just stared at them.

"And you still can't figure it out? You still think that I'm some street slut involved with a drug lord who's going to get locked up for a huge deal or maybe even for manufacturing and distributing drugs, once I testify?" She chuckled.

"She's a cop," Conway stated. She turned to look at him.

"Give the man a prize," she said and then stared at the men.

"You're law enforcement?" Lincoln asked.

She shoved her finger into Calder's chest and was filled with attitude.

"The name is Julianna Jacobs. My friends call me J.J. I'm an investigator for the Nevada State Police, and I work undercover for a special unit. Well, I did as of a month ago. Now, I'm a woman with a bull's-eye on my forehead, just trying to stay alive. My chances are slim. I get that, considering who's after me, but I've accepted it," she said and then looked away from the four of them. Before they could react, she turned back toward them.

"Hey, it is what it is. If it seems like these guys are coming this way, I'll get out of here on my own. I won't let you die because of me," she said and started to walk out of the room.

"So who is Frank?" Calder asked, with his arms crossed in front of his chest.

She stared at Calder. "Frank is my commander, and my only friend. He set this up. He contacted Sandman as a last resort to keep me alive. I pray that he isn't killed because of me."

She walked away and Conway looked at the men.

"I'll go talk to her. You guys get things started with dinner," Conway stated.

"No," Calder said. "It was me who got in her face and challenged her. I'll handle this."

Conway nodded his head as Calder left the room.

He looked at Brook and Lincoln.

"We were all way off," Brook stated.

"We sure the fuck were," Lincoln said.

"We need to get her to come around and give us more information on her situation. If she was working undercover, then more than likely she has evidence or actual proof to put away some seriously powerful people. If the federal agents who were watching her the first time around in protective custody were paid off and killed, then the person she has info against is very powerful and resourceful."

"So are we. She needs us, Conway. You saw her eyes. You heard the defeat in her voice. It's like she's accepted the fact that she's going to get killed by this guy. That really fucking pisses me off," Lincoln stated.

"Me, too. And it isn't just the fact that the four of us are totally attracted to her. She's like the perfect woman for the four of us," Brook stated. Conway shook his head and released a long sigh.

"That's another thing we're going to have to address later tonight, after she's gone to bed. But for now, let's just make her feel comfortable, and give her every opportunity to open up about herself, even if it means sharing some info on us."

"I'm all for that. She's been hurt badly enough. Those bruises are a reminder that whatever she went through it wasn't easy to escape from," Brook added.

"I feel an even stronger urge to protect her now. Call me crazy, but she's special," Lincoln said and then exited the room. Brook followed as Conway looked toward the hallway. Calder had entered J.J.'s room and she hadn't thrown him out yet. A good sign? He felt his own gut clench and hope fill him inside. No woman had given him such a jolt the way J.J. had tonight. Learning that she was an undercover investigator just added to her appeal. Conway knew that things happened for a reason. Her being sent here to them was not just coincidence. They were all suffering in their own ways. Whether it was fear of their pasts, fear of the present, or despair over feeling alone, even though the house was full.

Could J.J. change that for them? Could they protect her once they knew all the details of her case? Hope swelled inside of him as Conway headed into the kitchen, too.

* * * *

J.J. leaned against the window frame in her bedroom. She felt defeated, lost, and completely confused about what had just happened out there in the living room. She really had no qualms about telling the men about her life about what happened. But as Calder became confrontational, she'd done what she always did. She closed up, got in her fighting stance, and prepared to battle it out. But he was Special Forces. Was she losing her freaking mind?

She heard the knock on her door and before she could say come in, Calder entered. He walked right in and stopped in the middle of her room. Immediately having the man in her bedroom changed her emotions. He was six feet four, in phenomenal physical condition, and he was staring at her.

"Listen, I'm sorry for coming off so strong back there. I shouldn't have pushed."

"Calder, there's no need to apologize. I'm used to having to defend my capabilities, and especially with men. Don't sweat it. It will be cool from here on out," she said as she pushed off the windowsill and stood straight.

"You were upset, and I kept pushing."

She walked closer. "Calder, I don't need coddling. I'm used to doing things on my own, just as I'm sure you are. I could be a bit more understanding to your position and your team's as well. But I don't need sympathy or pampering," she said and started walking toward the doorway.

Calder grabbed her upper arm, stopping her directly in front of him. His eyes zeroed in on hers, as he stared down at her.

"Sympathy or pampering. Damn, why the hell are you so full of fucking attitude?"

"Me? What about you? You've been giving me shit since I got here. You're distrusting and bossy."

"You're distrusting, too," he countered.

"You're worse," she stated. Calder pulled her against him.

She gasped. "You have a real tough girl attitude, and that drives me fucking crazy."

They were both breathing rapidly. But J.J. felt this argument going in another direction, and so did her pussy. Her nipples hardened, her face felt flush.

"Fuck," Calder said, and then lifted her up and kissed her.

She immediately straddled his hips, as his large palm grabbed a hold of her ass. He kissed her deeply, as they both struggled for control of the kiss as their hands explored one another's bodies like wild animals.

His hands were big and hard as they grabbed at her body. She felt his one hand move under her blouse and the cami she wore and straight to her breast. He cupped it hard, and she moaned into his mouth. In a flash she was pressed up against the wall in the bedroom. She grabbed a hold of his head, feeling how hard and defined even his face and neck were.

They both pulled from their mouths at the same time to breathe. They were chin to chin and the power of their attraction was so intense they just stared at one another.

"Holy shit," he said.

"Exactly," she replied, and then he went after her neck. He licked and sucked her skin and collarbone and as he moved his lips across the front she gasped, grabbing his head to pull him back. The tears hit her eyes. She clenched them tightly. The damn bruising was still so raw and fragile.

"Shit. I'm sorry. Fuck," he whispered, as he slowly lowered her feet to the ground. She straightened out her blouse, and he fixed his shirt.

She thought for a moment that he was going to deny what had just happened between them. But he didn't.

Calder placed one hand over her shoulder above the wall behind her. His other hand held her hip in place as she leaned back against the wall. And his thigh remained between her legs and softly against her mound. Despite the jeans she wore, she knew she was dripping wet. Calder was one sexy, aggressive soldier.

He stared down at her as she gently held her throat.

"I'm sorry about that. We got a little carried away, huh?" He gave a small smile. She didn't know he had that in him. He was always so tough and serious all the time.

"No problem. I guess it's going to take some time for these bruises to heal completely."

He lifted his hand from her waist. She felt the loss but then he gently glided his thumb over her throat. He was very careful not to apply even the slightest bit of pressure. She could imagine him holding her throat gently, possessively, as he sunk his cock deep into her cunt. J.J. closed her eyes and willed away the desire.

"No one has ever gotten under my skin the way you have. Not one fucking person I've met," he told her. She opened her eyes, as his fingers left her throat and then trailed to her shoulder where he twirled part of her hair around his finger.

"What about Pauline?"

He snorted.

"I said under my skin, not on my nerves."

"Give me time. I'm sure I can accomplish that," she teased.

He nodded.

"I want to get to know you. I want to know the whole story, everything."

She felt herself tense up.

"Is that why you kissed me?" she asked. He gripped her hip and gave her a squeeze.

"Hell, no. I kissed you because I wanted to. Shit, J.J., you're damn lucky that everyone was in that room earlier, or I would have hauled your very naked ass over my shoulder and straight to my bedroom. We'd still be there now."

She felt her cheeks warm.

"Awfully cocky, aren't you, Calder?"

"Confident, ma'am. Cockiness gets people killed."

They stared at one another again, and she wondered what he was thinking.

"There's a lot for us to talk about. This thing, what just happened—"

"Is a mistake, and we shouldn't let it happen again."

"Hell, no. It wasn't a mistake. It is going to happen again, and I won't be the only one kissing these lips or exploring this body."

"What?" she asked filled with shock.

"You know damn well that you're attracted to all of us on the team. Just like we're all attracted to you. What you need to understand, is that things are going to change from here on out. You're going to explain everything so that we have the tools and the knowledge we need to protect you and help you. Keep an opened mind and just let it happen. After dinner, we'll start," he said and then pushed away from the wall. He took her hand and was leading her from the bedroom.

"Hey, I need to fix up or they're going to know that we kissed."

"Honey, they already know," he said as they headed down the hallway. She felt her cheeks warm up mighty damn fast and her belly tighten in fear before they reached the kitchen. How would they know? Would Conway and the others be angry, pissed off, confrontational? She just didn't think she could handle anything else tonight. When they entered the kitchen, all eyes were upon them.

J.J. swallowed hard as Calder held her by her hips and directed her toward her chair.

One glance around the room at Conway, Brook, and Lincoln, and she felt her temperature go up another notch. They weren't mad. Those weren't expressions of anger, disgust, or disappointment. No way. Instead, every feminine instinct told her exactly what was in their eyes.

Hunger.

* * * *

Long after J.J. went to bed, the men gathered around the surveillance room to talk about what had transpired. Conway was leading the discussion, taking his role as their team leader beyond the years in the field. He was good at it, and none of his team complained. He had some concerns about this job, and ultimately the way all his men immediately took to J.J. It was time to have a serious discussion.

"Okay, I understand that we discussed the possibility of sharing one woman, just like some of our close friends have. But what we need to discuss is number one, are we sure that we're ready to do something like this, now that we're face to face with a prospective candidate that we obviously mutually are attracted to, and secondly, why J.J.? What makes her stand out from any other women we've ever met since retiring from the military?" Conway asked.

He looked around the room and Brook very seriously began his perspective.

Brook was leaning back in the chair, his palms flat on his thighs as he looked at each of them and then back at Conway.

"Initially, she pissed me off. Her attitude sucked, and her refusal to even engage in a civilized conversation with any of us got to me. However, it was the lost look on her face, in those moments when she zones out, like we've all witnessed, that tugged at something deep within me. Maybe it's the artist in me, the craftsman that molds plain wood into something more, that makes me realize how beautiful J.J. truly is. Discard the bruises, the piss-fucking-poor attitude, and peel away those layers of distrust and fear, and look at her. She's everything each of us had discussed that we wanted in a woman."

"He's right. Everything Brook said is right on. She's scared, and those bruises on her neck indicate that her struggle to survive must have been frightening. Have you seen her neck up closely? There are finger marks there. Fucking finger marks, guys. Someone held that woman by her throat to try to kill her or control her. That just fucking pisses me off. She wants our help. I know she does. You heard our conversation in the gym. She asked a lot of questions about PTSS. She knows she has it and she's suffering from it. We can help her," Lincoln stated.

"J.J. is stubborn, she's used to handling things by herself and being left with nowhere to go, no one to trust, and being hunted like some fucking animal isn't right. She needs us. But to answer your question more directly, Conway, we need her. She's the first and only woman that the four of us met and that we all agree we want. She's got the tough no-nonsense attitude that I find pretty fucking sexy," Calder stated.

"No shit. That's why an argument between the two of you ended up with your tongue down her throat and her pinned against the bedroom wall," Lincoln retorted.

They all chuckled.

"She's not a pushover. This case she was working undercover on must be considered pretty high profile. I want her safe. I don't want her touched, bruised, hurt by another person again. If that's not good enough of an answer for any of you, then I don't care," Calder added.

"It's a good enough answer. It's what we're all thinking, besides the fact that she's got the sexiest body any of us have ever seen on a woman," Brook said.

"Well, at least one for real and not in between the pages of *Playboy*," Lincoln added. They laughed.

"What about you, Conway? You weren't too keen about engaging in this type of relationship when we started talking about the possibility years ago. What's changed?" Calder asked.

Conway took a deep breath as he leaned against the desk. He looked at his men, his team, his family.

"We did. The four of us have been together for most of our lives. We always have one another's backs. We feel safest together as a team. There are no secrets between us because we're one unit, one team, and together we're whole. That's with all our faults, our weaknesses, although we don't admit to those, and our strengths. We've gotten through some heavy shit in our lives, together. She doesn't have anyone. She's tough, but she still can't handle this alone. She can't keep up this pace of self-sacrifice. J.J. definitely does have all the qualities we said we wanted in a woman to share. She has more than all of them. She is beyond anything we could have conjured up in our minds. But my fear is for her sake. She's in over her head. She has already admitted that she believes death is coming. She's fragile.

Is it fair for us to pursue her romantically, when the woman is so scared and distrusting?"

"She needs us right now. She needs reassurance and support, but she needs honesty. We can't pretend that we don't want her in our bed, and between us. We can't lie to her and ignore these desires. It will cause trouble between all of us, and that could scare her even more. I say we let it happen. She's not going anywhere and neither are we. We take the time to get to know her, the situation, and how we all fit together. That's a normal process, Chief," Brook said and they chuckled.

Conway shook his head.

"Holy shit, when she called me chief like that, I was so tempted to throw her over my knee and spank that ass of hers. Fuck. She shocked me," Conway admitted.

They laughed.

"Well, it's how I wound up in a make out sessions with her," Calder stated.

"She may not be military, but as law enforcement she protects under similar rules. She helps to enforce the laws and keep people safe. I respect that. I consider her one of us, and we will find out her story. We need to. It can help us to protect her and it can help her to start healing," Conway added.

"I bet she looks fucking hot in a uniform," Brook stated.

"Hell, yeah, and even better out of it," Lincoln said.

"So we agree to take our time, get to know her, and let the cards fall?" Conway asked.

They all agreed.

"She'll come around. We'll find out who did this to her and we'll help put him away," Lincoln said.

"Six feet under sounds better to me," Calder added and they all agreed.

Chapter 5

J.J. was working out in the gym. She had already done the elliptical and now was moving around the punching bag. Lincoln and Calder were with her, as per their rules of her going nowhere without at least one of them.

No one mentioned last night, the kiss, or even asked her any questions at the dinner table. She had been shocked. It seemed that the tension was still high, but there was an added feel of anticipation. It had her walking on eggshells, but not the men. Long after she went to bed, the four of them remained up talking. Their mumbled voices eventually put her to sleep, as she thought about Calder and their little make out session.

Calder had the darkest gray eyes she had ever seen. But after they had kissed, the color seemed to brighten. She didn't know if she'd imagined it, but it was like he let his guard down for just a moment. Perhaps she was just desperate to feel like she wasn't so alone in her need to keep a distance and isolate herself. The four men, Calder, Lincoln, Brook, and Conway had a look in their eyes that was so similar it kind of bugged her out. They weren't brothers as far as she knew. At least in the biological sense or through blood, but there was a definite bond there.

Recalling Anthony and his good friends from his troop, they shared a lot, and had been there for her when he died, but they had a lot of their own issues, and J.J. was always trying to prove herself and come across so independent and capable. Now suddenly, she was feeling needy.

She didn't like this feeling. She didn't want to be weak or unable to stand on her own. But the anxiety and paranoia was getting worse. Any sound, any indication of a possible attack, set her off. Maybe it was because she had been on edge for over a month now. Maybe surviving multiple attacks, and witnessing a rape and murder, had placed her into this emotional and psychological turmoil? Post-traumatic stress did this kind of stuff to people. But she was a cop, a trained investigator, who'd gone through rigorous training and psychological evaluations before being accepted into the Nevada State Police investigation unit. Perhaps the last four years of her life had finally caught up with her?

Thinking back to when she was with Calder, she remembered feeling safe. If she was at all honest with herself, she felt safe around all of them, even now, in the gym. But at night, alone in bed, she was alert, on edge, and ready to pull her gun from under her pillow and take an attacker down, even if it was the last thing she did.

At some point she had dozed off, but soon awoke in a cold sweat, shaking like a leaf. She knew it was getting worse. But she didn't know what to do about it. She debated asking one of the guys. They had been through war, had experienced intense situations, and perhaps even faced death head-on as Special Forces, and maybe they could help? As she thought about it more, she denied herself the weakness of asking for help from them. This wasn't that bad. A touch of post-traumatic stress syndrome along with fear of being caught, tortured, and killed would probably make anyone uptight and jittery.

But the visions in her nightmares, and they were definitely nightmares, were so vivid and real. She felt each strike to her flesh, each cut of the blade, and the feel of the breath leaving her body as Dexter choked her.

She suddenly felt the tap to her arm, and so deep in morbid, fearful thought, she reacted. Like a trained fighter, she ducked and then struck.

The moment her gloved hand hit Brook in the stomach, she gasped and then turned away from him.

"Oh, God, I'm sorry, Brook. I'm so sorry."

Someone placed their hands on her shoulders and she turned out of the hold. It was Lincoln, and now Brook joined him next to her.

"Hey, no apology necessary. I snuck up on you, I guess," he said, eyeing her over and appearing as if he wanted to say more.

"I didn't even think. I just...I'm sorry," she said, and looked away from him.

Shit, they're going to think I'm violent and that I don't want them touching me. Well, I shouldn't want them touching me.

"We called your name, but you didn't hear us. You were in a dead stare at the punching bag," Brook stated.

"No, I wasn't. I was hitting it. I was focused on what I was doing," she said. Lincoln looked at Brook and then back at her.

"What? I said I was sorry. What do you want me to do?" she snapped at Brook, and then started to walk away. Brook grabbed her hand to stop her. She stopped and looked up at him.

"What were you thinking about?" he asked, very seriously.

She gave a fake chuckle. "Hitting the bag. That's what I was doing." She tried to pull her hand free but now Lincoln placed his hand on her waist.

"Baby, you were staring into outer space, and then you looked so frightened, and you were shaking." She pulled away from them.

"No. No I wasn't, I was fine. I am fine," she said, raising her voice.

"You weren't fine. Just like you're not fine at night, when you wake up screaming or gasping for air," Lincoln yelled at her as he stepped toward her.

She saw red. She was so angry. *Was he spying on me?*

"You bastard." She swung at him, and he ducked and then countered. She ducked and it began, a crazy sparring match based on her anger and refusal to ask for help or to admit that her sessions of zoning out were getting the better of her.

"Come on. Get it out. You're all filled with piss and vinegar, and I'm ready for it. Come on. This makes you feel happy. Denying what's going on here is working for you?" He egged her on and she swung her arms and hands at Lincoln until he grabbed her, did a quick maneuver, and tackled her rather gently to the mat. He was over her body, had her arms pinned above her head, and he was using his thick, hard, long legs to hold her in place.

She held his gaze and she was the one breathing heavily. Lincoln hadn't even broken a sweat. Her nostrils filled with his cologne, and the soap they all used.

Her shirt was lifted up to her breasts, her spankies shorts rode up her very sensitive, throbbing cunt, and this damn model of a soldier was just staring at her.

"Have you had enough?" he asked.

"No," she yelled.

"Honey, I think you should know that Calder and Lincoln are training instructors for law enforcement in self-defense and hand-to-hand combat. We're all highly trained."

She eased her legs in just the right position below Lincoln and gave a soft smile as she weakened her grip. He in return eased up, as she slid her leg seductively up and down his thigh. "Hand-to-hand combat, huh?" she asked in a seductive whisper.

Lincoln's green eyes sparkled as he eased his hold, and then she prepared to make her move.

"So am I," she said and then used all her might to take Lincoln's one leg out from under him, causing him to fall to the right, so she could shove all her strength that way. She did, and wound up straddling him. But Lincoln countered the move and they rolled across the mat, slamming one another down each time. Finally Lincoln held her down, using one hand to grip her wrists above her head, while he pressed his pelvis between her thighs making her widen her legs and straddle him.

She tried pressing her thighs against his ribs but then the sneak began tickling her with one hand. His fingers were everywhere. Under her shirt, over her breasts, and then between her thighs as she laughed and screamed for mercy.

"Mercy! Mercy, I give. Oh, God!"

Lincoln stopped and she locked gazes with him right before his mouth crushed down onto hers.

* * * *

Lincoln was so fired up. He felt aggressive, possessive, emotionally attached, and he damn well shouldn't. As far as he could tell, J.J. was suffering from some serious post-traumatic stress. She was denying it, wouldn't ask for help, and he was losing his patience. They'd talked about it last night, after she'd gone to bed. They'd also talked about wanting her, and the attraction they felt. It was decided to just let things ride, but today, things were different.

Her attitude, the fact that she'd zoned out again in front of him and Brook was upsetting and concerning. She was literally fighting for her independence and didn't realize that they could be trusted. He and Brook would show her, and so would Conway and Calder.

As she'd pulled the move on him, making him tumble to the right, he was pleasantly surprised. The woman had guts, and she was definitely physically fit. The sight of her on her back, the sound of her laughing as he tickled her, and the swell of her large breasts beneath the tank she wore, was too much to ignore. Throw in what looked to be a tattoo on her hipbone, and damn, he wanted a taste of her, and now he had his chance.

He slowly released his hold on her wrists, as he explored her mouth. J.J. was kissing him back, and the legs that were squeezing his ribs a few moments ago were now snug against him. He pressed the hair from her face, and eased his lips from hers. He kissed the corner of her mouth, then trailed lower. He didn't go near her bruises, knowing that they still hurt, and that Calder had kissed her there and found out. He pressed her tank up higher, as he scooted lower and kissed her belly. The small gold hoop was a surprise too as he licked her belly button and tapped the jewelry. She gripped his hair.

"Oh, God, Lincoln. What the hell is happening? We have to stop."

"No, you don't. It's too fucking hot to stop," Brook said, and J.J. gasped as she tuned to look at him.

"I think Brook feels left out, baby," Lincoln stated and then jumped up in one move, and reached a hand down to her. She took his hand, looking at Lincoln and then back at Brook.

The moment she was standing up straight, Lincoln turned her around, wrapped an arm around her midsection, and kissed the side of her neck.

"He wants to taste you, too. You're too damn sexy for us to not want you."

J.J. rolled her head back against Lincoln's shoulder as Brook stepped closer. She was sandwiched between them.

Brook placed his palm against her cheek and stared down into her eyes. "You're so beautiful. You've got a hell of a temper, baby. A hell of a temper," Brook said against her lips right before he kissed her.

Lincoln eased back slightly but moved his hand upward to cup her breast as Brook devoured her moans. This situation was like nothing they'd ever experienced before. They knew that they wanted to share a woman, and have the kind of relationship their friends like Sandman and his brothers had with Grace. They'd had had sex with the same woman a couple of times but never together. One by one, but it was never all four of them together. Maybe two of them and then the other two afterward or even alone. But with J.J., Lincoln could see all of them taking her together, in the same room, the same bed.

She was moaning now, and pushing her chest against Lincoln's hand while Brook continued to kiss her. She felt so good in Lincoln's arms, and by the way Brook was kissing her and exploring her body with his hands, he must have thought she felt really good, too.

"What the hell kind of workout is this?"

J.J. pulled from Brook's kiss as Conway entered the dojo.

She quickly tried to separate from Brook and Lincoln, but neither man let her. Lincoln smiled.

"J.J.'s got quite a temper on her, and some really good moves," he said.

"She sure does. She pulled one on Lincoln, surprising him. I think she's filled with surprises," Brook said as he stroked the back of his hand down her cheek.

Conway walked closer. He was dressed in light sweats and a tank top.

"Is she really that good?" Conway asked, not taking his eyes off of J.J.

"I'd say so, and tastes really good, too. But don't take my word for it," Brook said and then stepped away. Conway took his place.

* * * *

Conway was in the surveillance room with Calder, going over some information on the computer of any recent major crimes or trials going before a judge in Nevada. They caught sight of a few things that peaked their interest, but it was the flat screen monitors of the dojo that immediately caught their eyes, as well as a very fired up brunette.

Conway couldn't stay back there and watch Brook and Lincoln make out with J.J. He wanted to be sure a real attraction was there, and not just one stemming from watching two of his closest friends get it on with one sexy investigator.

Conway placed his hand against her cheek and J.J.'s eyes widened.

"You getting a good workout in, J.J.?" he asked as he gently rubbed her bottom lip with his thumb. Her lips were red and swollen, well kissed by Brook and Lincoln, and soon by him, too. She had luscious lips and big green eyes that currently looked aroused.

"Not bad," she replied in challenge and Lincoln pulled her back against his chest. She gasped and then closed her eyes. One look downward and Conway saw Lincoln's hand cupping her mound over the thin spankies shorts she wore.

"You like how that feels, J.J.? You like Lincoln caressing that pussy while I watch?"

She popped her eyes open.

Lincoln shifted his hand up, and then under the spandex of her shorts. He delved his fingers deep and she jerked forward.

"Now there's no barrier. I like this a lot better. Your pussy is all hot and wet, baby. You like this, don't you?" Lincoln asked. His mouth was on her neck and shoulder and his fingers were down her shorts.

Conway held her chin between his fingers, as he stepped closer. She was softly moaning, but held Conway's gaze.

"Looks like there's going to be a lot of changes around here, J.J. In case you didn't realize it, we're all interested in getting to know you," he said.

"Oh, God, Lincoln, please. Conway, I can't take it."

"You will," both Conway and Lincoln said, and then Conway covered her mouth and kissed her. Her hands came up quickly and grabbed on to his shoulders. He could feel her fingernails collide against his scalp, as they dueled for control of the kiss. She tasted so good, so incredible he wanted to fast-forward and just get her in his bed and fuck her until she was totally his. It was obscene and wild the way she made him feel.

He continued to kiss her while Lincoln thrust his fingers up into her pussy. She was countering back, thrusting her hips forward, when she pulled her mouth from Conway's and growled her release. She shook and then fell forward against Conway's chest, with Lincoln still holding on to her, too.

Conway looked at Lincoln, whose face was all scrunched up and red. He looked wild and hungry. Conway knew exactly how he felt.

"It's okay, baby. We've got you," he said as Lincoln caressed her hair, and Conway held her against his chest.

Lincoln slowly pulled his hand form her pants and stepped back. He placed his hands on his upper thighs as he bent over, catching his breath or simply recovering from the scene.

Conway smirked.

"She's incredible."

"She sure is."

Conway pressed the palms of his hands against her cheek as he stared down into her eyes. She looked so content and sexy.

"Easy now, baby. Can you walk, or can I carry you?"

She rolled her eyes.

"I'm able to walk. It's just been a while."

"I'd love to hear more about that," Lincoln stated, following her from the mats.

"I wouldn't. I don't want to hear about her with anyone else," Brook chimed in as Conway placed his hands on her shoulders, walking out of the dojo behind her.

"Just forget about it. This is crazy enough. Now all I need is to see Calder," she said as they walked across the yard and headed into the house. As they entered the kitchen, there was Calder, his expression firm, as he pointed at J.J. and curled his finger at her indicating for her to come to him.

She crossed her arms in front of her chest and stared at him as if he were out of his mind. Conway and the others chuckled.

"Unless you want that spanking right here in the middle of the kitchen, I suggest you get over here right now."

Conway felt the excitement and sexual energy attack his senses. He could see J.J. naked and spread over the edge of the table as they each spanked her sexy ass. That would send him over the edge.

She looked over her shoulder at them, and their expressions must have been obvious indicators of what they were all thinking. She walked toward Calder, and right into his arms. He wrapped her in his embrace, placing his palm over her ass cheek before he leaned down and kissed her deeply. They all watched, all in awe of the connection and attraction they had, with hopes of it progressing.

J.J. reached up and wrapped her arms around Calder's neck as he lifted her up, turned her around, and placed her ass on the kitchen counter. He pressed his thighs between hers and she straddled him while they made out in the kitchen without a care of the audience behind them.

"I think lunch is on hold," Brook teased.

"I think J.J. is lunch," Conway said, and they all chuckled as Calder gave the thumbs-up while he continued to kiss J.J.

* * * *

J.J. was in a daze. She'd just made out with four different men in a matter of minutes.

Four, totally sexy, muscular, military men who affected her like no one ever had before. Not even Anthony.

She closed her eyes and lowered her head. *Anthony. God, I thought I would never get over him, or how suddenly I lost him. Why do I feel guilty? I have nothing to feel guilty about. He's been dead for a while now. I cut off everyone, every man who ever hit on me since. Why am I accepting these four men right now. Four?*

Calder cupped her chin.

"Hey now, don't go overthinking this and freaking out. It was bound to happen. The attraction was instant. We all know this, J.J."

She tried to get down but he wouldn't let her.

"Don't push us away. Just slow down and stop running."

He was right. She was running. From her past, from her fears, her guilt. All of it.

She shook her head.

"I'm not ready for this. I don't know what to think of this, or why it feels so right and why I feel so wrong."

He caressed her cheek, as the others stood around him, watching her. She looked at them. They were all so big, so serious and determined looking.

"We're going to take this slow," Conway stated firmly from the left side, next to Calder.

She chuckled.

"Take things slow?" she asked, and now Conway placed his hand on her hair by her ear and cheek, and gently stroked her skin. His dark brown eyes and deep expression unnerved her. The fact that two men touched her at once, while two more stood nearby ready to touch her too was shocking. She felt the connection, that stir of something amazing deep in her gut. She nearly shivered from the effects of it.

Her lips parted. She could feel him, them, and this overwhelming sensation to let go. "Oh, God," she whispered, releasing a breath. Conway continued to stroke her cheek as Calder caressed her thighs, spreading them wider.

"We feel it, too," Conway whispered.

"Fucking crazy," Calder added.

"Bring her into the bedroom. Your bedroom, Conway," Lincoln stated. Or rather commanded from behind them. She looked toward him and Brook. Both men removed their shirts, and damn, were they beautiful. But they seemed to react to Lincoln's words. They all exchanged glances.

"Bring her," Brook said.

"Agreed," Calder whispered, still holding her gaze.

"Agreed," Conway whispered. She licked her lower lip and pulled it between her teeth. Why did it sound like some sort of plan was in motion? The way they said "agreed" triggered something instinctual in her.

"Baby, you're killing me here," Calder told her, and then thrust softly against her mound. She felt his hard cock and knew he wanted to have sex with her, so did the others. Was there some sort of significance with bringing her to Conway's room?

Is that where they brought the women they shared?

Would she be just another woman they seduced with their charms, their bodies, and large attitudes?

Did she even care?

She thought about that a moment.

Nope. Not a care at all right now. I want them. I want to feel connected. I want to feel beautiful and real. I want to feel alive, even if the near future brings my death.

Calder lifted her up off the counter, as if she were light as a feather, and carried her out of the room. The others followed.

"Uhm, where are we going? Why Conway's room? What does it mean?" she asked, feeling panicky. No one answered, and then they were down another hallway. It was an area of the house she hadn't been to. Conway opened the door, and J.J. looked at Calder.

"It's where you belong, the first time and every time." He kissed her as he lowered her feet to the rug. That kiss took over every ounce of her being. She barely felt the hands under her shirt, lifting it up to get it over her head. Calder released her lips momentarily as someone pulled off the top. She heard compliments about her breasts, her bra, and body. She stared up at Calder.

"You're beautiful." He kissed her again. Their lips met and parted and then met and parted again, as if they were longtime lovers and couldn't seem to get enough of their lips.

Large, nimble fingers undid the clasp to her bra. She grabbed at it before it fell, and then her shorts were pressed down.

She felt that battle within her to give in or to fight, opening up herself to the vulnerability she knew would come from their encounter.

"Baby, relax and just feel. We promise to take good care of you," Conway told her. She locked gazes with him.

"I...I don't know if I can let go," she whispered and a tear rolled down her cheek.

Calder pulled her against him and hugged her tight. The feel of his big strong arms holding her, and the fact that he stopped everything to console her, take care of her, was an indicator of his affection. At least she hoped that her gut was right. She squeezed him tight. The feel of hard, male flesh and its stereotypical benefits filled her feminine soul. To feel so instantly protected and cared for was one thing, but to not feel alone made her gasp. She felt the tension in her throat, the way her breathing grew rapid, and she started to panic.

Calder pulled back and caressed the hair from her cheeks. Her eyes darted around the room. It was a fight or flight sensation as she tried to move away from him.

"Look at me. Look at me, J.J.," he demanded. She fought his control. She closed her eyes and she saw Dexter.

"Oh, God," she stated aloud.

"It's Calder, no one else. Open your eyes and see that it's me, baby. Come on now. Look at me, not through me. You can do it, J.J. I know that you can."

His voice was soothing, but his tone firm. She stared into his dark eyes, almost black in color. They were piercing and strong, just like Calder.

She heard her own shaky rapid breath, and then felt the hands on her shoulders.

"Easy. Just breathe, baby. Remember where you are and hold on to that thought. Look at Calder. Look into his eyes and focus on him. Relax your breathing, baby. I'm right here, too. I'm behind you," Conway said as he gently caressed her shoulders as he pressed his front to her back. She was sandwiched between them and their masculine warmth. She felt cocooned. Then she felt Brook on one side, and Lincoln on the other side. They were all so close to her. The heat of their bodies, the tone of their voices, and the way they came to her aid at once overwhelmed her.

"I'm getting there. I'm so sorry. I don't know why this keeps happening," she said and felt her body begin to shake. Calder wrapped his arms around her and someone grabbed a blanket and covered her body.

She shoved at their hands.

"No. No, I'm not cold at all. I'm hot, and damn it, I want this. I want you," she said to Calder. "I want all of you. Just make it stop. Please. Make it stop."

She shrugged her shoulders making the blanket fall from her body. She continued to shake as she reached up, running her hands up and over Calder's shoulders before standing up on tiptoes to kiss him.

She felt Conway's hands on her back, and Brook's on her pants, while Lincoln kissed the skin on her hipbone on one side of her.

She pressed her tongue deeper into Calder's mouth and felt the shivering subside. She put all her energy into this moment, this time with these men who obviously empathized with her state of mind, her emotions and fears. Knowing that they suffered from the same type of issue in their lives caused some kind of imaginary bond between the five of them. They did things together as a unit. They would do her as a unit, too. She wanted to be part of them in every way.

Calder's large hands caressed over her skin. They parted lips and he smiled at her.

"You are everything and then some," he said, making her cheeks warm and her nipples harden.

"Don't be shy with us. We're going to take good care of you," Conway whispered from behind her. She felt his hands smooth under her arms and over her breasts. The bra fell from her hands as the sensation of Conway's large, callused fingers massaged her needy breasts. He pulled on the nipples simultaneously, sending a jolt of cream to hit her cunt.

"That's a lovely sound. You moaning and gasping from our touch," Conway told her and then licked along her neck as he continued to massage her breasts.

"Is that a tattoo and a belly ring?" Brook asked. She popped her eyes open in time to see him kneel down next to her and place his hard, warm hand over her lower belly and mound as he stared at the tattoos. It was a small shooting star.

Brook's hands were large, his fingers long and thick. They looked so big over her skin. It was masculine and made her feel feminine. How silly.

His thumb caressed over it, and then she felt the lips against her belly. There was Lincoln. He was kissing her skin, making his way toward her mound with his lips and tongue. Brook lifted her thigh. He placed it on his knee, spreading her open for Lincoln. Conway grabbed her, using his hold on her breasts and his solid, hard chest to keep her from losing her balance.

"You're already so wet, baby. God, that makes me happy," Lincoln whispered then stroked his fingers over her pussy lips.

"Keeping us happy in here is a good thing," Conway whispered, then nipped her neck. She shivered with anticipation and excitement.

"This is torture," she said, sounding breathless.

"This is where nothing else matters but us. You, me, Calder, Brook, and Lincoln. No one else, nothing else," Conway said as he pulled on her nipples, just as Lincoln pressed two fingers up into her pussy. Brook licked across her hipbone and over the tattoo. He nibbled on the bone on her hip, making her pussy leak some more.

"You taste incredible. I can't wait to be inside of you," Brook told her.

"Me either. I'm ready, is she?" Calder asked. She heard his voice coming from behind them. Slowly Lincoln pulled his fingers from her cunt and then leaned forward and licked her pussy. He began to eat at her cream, nip her clit, and twirl his tongue around her pussy.

"Oh, Lincoln. Oh, God, I'm coming." She moaned, and he stopped. He pulled his mouth from her cunt and stood up.

"What the hell?" she stated.

"You come when we tell you that you can." Conway pinched her again and then released her breasts. Brook stood up, turned her around, and marched her forward. There was Calder. He was lying on the biggest bed she had ever seen. It was covered with pillows and a thick, fluffy, hunter-green comforter. It looked so comfortable and like something out of a fantasy story. She chuckled. It was so appropriate. This was a fantasy. It couldn't really be happening.

"Are you on the pill?" Brook asked as he lifted her up and right onto Calder. He was lying on the edge of the bed, completely naked, and his big, long hard dick pointing upward.

She was in shock as her flesh hit his flesh. Her thighs pressed against his muscular thighs, and she felt so aroused and excited. She ran the palms of her hands up his very muscular thighs in admiration. Calder grabbed her hips and lifted her up. She fell to his chest.

"Well? Pill or no pill?" Calder asked. She just stared at him. The man was a work of art.

Smack.

She gasped and turned not expecting the smack to her backside.

She stared at Conway.

"You were asked a question."

"No. I'm not on anything."

"We got it covered," Brook said and then moved around the room. A moment later, Calder was pulling her down to kiss her. She hugged him hard. She hadn't been with a man in almost three years.

She absorbed the feel of thick, steel-hard male flesh beneath her breasts, her hands, and pussy. She straddled him as best she could, and kissed him back, giving him as good as he was giving her. He had ridges and dips in his flesh from all the hard muscles. He had muscles where she never knew muscles existed.

He released her lips and lifted her up.

"Put this on him," Conway stated, joining them on the bed. He was naked, too, and damn, was he just as well built as Calder. His cock was huge and thick. His skin a bit tanner than Calder's and his expression was firm as usual.

Calder cupped her breasts and she grabbed on to his chest for support. Conway placed his hand over one of her hands. He turned it over and placed the foil wrapper into her palm. Then he cupped the back of her head, brought her closer to him, and kissed her.

She felt her pussy leak and her nipples harden. She was going to do this. She was naked, surrounded by four men with huge cocks that all wanted her. How could this be happening? When would it go wrong?

Conway released her lips.

"Put it on him. Tonight is a very special night. We're going to make you forget about everything but us," Conway whispered.

She felt the force of his words.

She fumbled with the foil. She hadn't opened one of these in ages. She tore it open and pulled out the condom. She stared at Calder's cock.

"Put it on. You know how to, right?" he teased.

"It's been forever," she whispered and slowly moved toward his dick.

Calder grabbed her wrist as she pressed the contraceptive over his shaft and into position. "God, your touch is like fire. Take me, J.J. Lift up, take me inside of you and ride me. I need you."

She hesitated only a moment as she lifted up. She felt her thighs shaking. Her hands were, too, as she placed one hand on Calder's shoulder and the other on his encased cock, lining it up with her oversensitive pussy. She lifted higher, his cock thick and long, and then slowly lowered onto his shaft.

"Fuck, baby, you're so fucking tight. You're like a goddamn vise grip. Shit." He growled and then grabbed on to her hips and pumped upward. She gasped and fell forward, grabbing on to his chest.

"She's so damn tight. My God, I can hardly move."

"Oh, please move. Please, do something. You're so big and thick. Oh God, I don't know if I can take you," she stated, and then lifted up and tried to ease back down. But Calder was on a mission to penetrate deeper.

"Oh!" she screamed and then she felt the hands on her back, and something cold against her ass.

"What is that?" She moaned as Calder pumped his hips up and down, penetrating her, and lubricating her pussy with every stroke.

She looked over her shoulder, and Lincoln was there. He was pressing something to her ass.

"Oh, my God. What are you doing? Oh!" She moaned from the sensations. His fingers pressed something cold into her ass. She was relieved and amazed that it had made her instantly come and allowed Calder to penetrate all the way inside of her cunt. She'd never done anything so crazy. Sure, she'd thought about trying it, but held off. It was so forbidden and naughty and… "Oh!" she moaned again.

"I'm just getting this beautiful ass ready. My God, J.J., you have an outstanding ass," Lincoln stated and then pinched her ass cheeks. His words, his actions, along with Calder's thrusts, made her scream her orgasm. Calder followed.

"Holy God. Holy shit," he repeated and she lowered to his chest as Calder hugged her.

She squeezed him tightly as her body shivered with the aftereffects of their lovemaking. But what had shocked her, what had amazed her and nearly brought tears to her eyes, was the feeling Calder's hug alone had caused inside of her. She could love a man like Calder. Just as she could love Conway, Brook, and Lincoln. That scared the crap out of her.

How could she love four men at once? How could four men love her and cherish her, alone?

They can't, you idiot. Take this for what it is. Lust, passion, and a human need to connect after being alone for so very long.

* * * *

The moment Lincoln placed his hands on her shoulders, J.J. jerked up and off of Calder. Conway was there to catch her and pull her into his arms.

"Whoa, baby, slow down. You're okay," Conway whispered, as he rolled her to her back and held her face between his hands. She was panting, and then swallowed hard.

Lincoln climbed up next to her. "I didn't mean to scare you. God, J.J., you're so skittish, baby. Don't you realize yet, that none of us would ever hurt you?" he asked.

She blinked her eyes.

"I'm scared," she whispered.

Lincoln looked at Conway. Conway lifted up, still straddling her waist, and held her face between his hands.

"You think we're not?"

She blinked, as if shocked by Conway's admittance.

"You? No," she whispered.

"You think we do this all the time? You think we open up our hearts, our bed, to just any woman?" he asked, feeling himself begin to get angry with her. Did she think that they were a bunch of male sluts?

"I guess I did. I mean, Pauline indicated—"

"Pauline is a fucking liar. She doesn't matter. She was never here, in this room, with all four of us. Never," Lincoln stated firmly. She looked at him and then back at Conway.

"I've never done anything like this in my life. I've never had anal sex before either. I don't have the experience you do," she stated in a shy voice.

Conway gave her a wink. "That's good to know. It makes you and us together, even more special. I want you, J.J. I want you like Calder just had you, and so do Brook and Lincoln. We won't hurt you. We'll put you first, always," Conway told her and when she nodded her head, he leaned down and kissed her.

When she placed her hands against Conway's, he released an emotion of relief inside. Little did she know that they had never shared a woman together, and that when Brook said to bring her to Conway's room, it meant that he was being the first to claim that J.J. was the woman they were waiting for. The one who touched their hearts and affected them way before they'd even made love to her.

J.J. was kissing him back, and pressing her hands along his muscles. Conway maneuvered his leg between hers and rolled over, so that she straddled him. Her long brown hair swayed over her shoulders, covering her breasts as he released her lips.

Her lovely face was flushed, her chest blotchy, and her nipples hard as pebbles.

"Condom?" she whispered, and he smiled.

"You sure you're ready?"

"Yes, Conway. As crazy as this all is, I want you, I want all of you. I feel so needy and I don't know if it's just from being alone for so long, or the power of what's happening here. But I want it."

"I want you, too, J.J.," Lincoln whispered as he took her hand, brought it to his lips, and kissed her fingertips. Conway watched as J.J. and Lincoln held gazes. The anticipation and the fear hit Conway in an instant. Would she allow them to make love to her together?

"You're a big man, Lincoln," she whispered, and then lowered her eyes to Lincoln's cock.

"You do it to me, baby. You've made me harder than I ever remember being in my life."

She licked her lower lip and took the condom from Lincoln's hand.

"Then I guess since I'm responsible for it. I should help any way I can."

Conway caressed up her ribs to her breasts and cupped them.

She closed her eyes and moaned, as Lincoln pressed a palm against her cheek, leaned over, and kissed her deeply.

In a flash that kiss grew sexy as damn hell. Conway was amazed as J.J. ripped open the condom and took hold of his cock, while still kissing Lincoln.

When she wrapped her fingers around his shaft, Conway moaned.

"Damn, woman, your hand feels so good wrapped around my cock."

Lincoln released her lips. He held a fistful of her hair and stared straight at her.

"I'm going to get your ass ready, and Conway and I are going to fuck you so good, and bind us as one."

"Yes," she whispered, and Conway got up off the bed.

"Let's get you ready," Conway told her as he scooted down lower on the bed so that his legs hung over and so did J.J.'s ass. She moaned as she placed the condom over his shaft. She rolled it down, her fingers sending jolts of desire straight to his balls.

She lifted up and eased her wet pussy down. Conway held her hips as their gazes locked.

"You are one sexy, hot woman."

"And you're one sexy, hot chief of police."

He chuckled as he gripped her hips and thrust upward.

She gasped and then leaned down and kissed him hard on the mouth. She was running her fingers through his hair, as he wrapped his arms around her, pressing his palm over her lower back and ass. She climbed up higher, spreading her thighs wider as she countered his thrusts.

The moment Lincoln touched her from behind, she slowed down.

"Nice and easy, baby. Don't mind me. You just keep pleasuring the chief," Lincoln said and a couple of chuckles went through the room.

* * * *

J.J. felt so wired right now. She couldn't seem to get enough of Conway, or relieve the sensation burning in her cunt. With every thrust it felt as if it grew deeper and a greater need grew inside of her.

She felt the cool liquid against her puckered hole again and pulled her mouth from Conway's.

"Easy now, baby. Just relax, and let it happen," Conway said. She laid her face against the crook in Conway's neck, and felt her breath get caught in her throat. She was oversensitive now. She zoned in on the feel of Conway's thick, hard cock deep inside her pussy, the way his warm, large palm stretched across her lower back and ass, and how Lincoln's fingers felt as they pushed through the tight rings and instantly brought a burning then pleasurable sensation.

Conway's strong arms held her as he thrust upward.

"Your ass is so beautiful. I love that my one hand can expand over most of it," Lincoln stated and then caressed her ass cheek as he thrust his fingers in her ass.

J.J. lifted up, against Conway's hold, and thrust back. "Oh, God, please, Lincoln. I need."

Conway moved his hands up her hips and back to her face and head. He cupped her there and stared into her eyes.

"We know exactly what you need," Conway said.

Lincoln pulled his fingers from her ass, and she felt the loss as she moaned and then pushed back again.

Lincoln's palm was on her ass then over her hip. She felt the tip of his cock against the sacred bud.

"This is fucking perfect. Here I come, baby. Here I come," Lincoln said and she tightened up as she closed her eyes. She felt nothing.

No one moved, and she popped her head up and stared at Conway. He was shaking his head at her as if reprimanding her. "Tsk, tsk, tsk. No tightening up. This is not to cause you pain, but to bring you pleasure. You want this, remember? You feel that deep hunger and need inside, don't you, baby?" Conway asked and then pulled on her nipple. She parted her lips and relaxed her belly and ass.

"Feel it? Chase after that hunger and take all that you can," he whispered and then thrust upward. She tried to calm her breathing and focus on the sensations instead of the fear of the unknown.

"Nice and easy," Lincoln told her. The feel of his long hard fingers massaging her ass cheeks, combined with Conway's thrusts, had her moaning and releasing her own cream.

"Oh," she moaned.

"Ride him. Rock those hips and take his cock as deep as you can," Lincoln said, and she did. She rose up and then lowered back down taking him to her womb. Up and down she continued to try and scratch that itch, that hunger she was getting closer and closer to but not reaching. Her breasts were moving with every thrust, and she felt so sexy and alive with desire.

She felt the bulbous tip of Lincoln's cock at her anus and then him slowly push through.

"Oh, God. Oh, my God!" She moaned and then slowly moved back against Lincoln's cock.

"Beautiful. Your ass is taking my cock all the way in, baby. Keep it up. Take what you need. Fuck," Lincoln blurted out as he held on to her shoulders. Conway pressed up and J.J. pressed down and back.

There was a shift in thought in her mind. She wanted to please them. She wanted these strong, muscular, sexually stimulating men deep inside of her. She wanted to bond, to make love, and complete the trio they were building.

Back and forth she tried to take both men deeper. She was losing focus, the sensations rocking her body and causing an eruption of sorts inside of her.

"Too fucking tight. Oh Fuck. I can't go slow. I can't," Lincoln ground out through what sounded like clenched teeth.

"Then don't. Fuck me harder, Lincoln, Conway. Take all of me. I need it. I need this," she said, and Lincoln kissed her shoulder before he grabbed on to her hips and thrust into her ass, balls deep. She was panting for air as the two men countered their strokes. One would shove in as one shoved out, making her long for both of them together. In and out they alternated thrusts. She felt every inch of their cocks enter her and then pull out. Her pussy felt so swollen and then there was this deep sensation and she knew if they just kept moving, she would reach that point of no return.

"Faster. Oh, God, don't stop. Please don't stop," she told them and both men picked up the pace. She moaned along with them. They called her name, as they pumped their hips. She felt their hands everywhere and she felt on the edge of something wonderful. She moved with them, countering their strokes until her body tightened like a bow and she exploded in pure bliss.

Conway thrust upward and came soon after her, calling her name as he pulled her down and nuzzled her neck. The move made her thighs spread wider and Lincoln slapped her ass as he fucked her harder and faster. She was so damn wet, and the orgasm just kept going and going, when finally Lincoln came hard and furious, calling her name. "J.J.!"

Her ears were ringing, and she could hardly concentrate on the movement around the room. She felt Lincoln kiss her shoulder and then pull slowly from her body. Conway rolled her to her side, pulling from her pussy and cupping her breast.

"Amazing. That was so amazing."

She stared at him, her heart racing, her body a bit sore. "I don't think I can move." They chuckled.

"I've got you, baby. I get to take care of you now," Brook said. She turned to look at him. Big wide shoulders, muscles galore, trailed down to a narrow waist with ridges of stomach muscles. His brown hair and deep brown eyes held her gaze as he smiled. "Come on. My turn to make love to you." He scooped her up into his arms and carried her out of the room. She laid her head against his chest as she looked at the others. They were all watching her, and they all looked so happy, it scared her. She didn't want them to get hurt. She wanted them safe. What if she just made matters worse?

* * * *

Brook started the shower after he set J.J. down on the counter on top of a towel.

After getting all the showerheads into position, lower so that they would reach J.J. perfectly, he stood in front of her. She immediately placed her hands on his chest and ran her palms over his muscles.

"You look tired," he told her.

"You'd be, too," she said and then winked. He smiled. Trailing a finger along her collarbone and down her arm, he thought she had an amazing body, like that of the perfect sculpture. Her defined arms, large breasts, and flat belly were very sexy.

"I love the feel of your skin and touching your curves." He cupped her breast and stared at the nipple, before tugging it.

"You have a great body, too, Brook. So many muscles," she said and then ran her palms over his skin. His cock jerked upward.

"I need you."

She turned to look down on the counter to where the condom package sat. Lifting it up, she smiled at him.

"I need you, too," she whispered.

He took the condom from her hands, opened it, and then placed it on his shaft. He lifted her up and kissed her hard on the mouth as she straddled his waist. Walking to the right, he stepped into the oversized shower, and the warm water sprayed their flesh. She pulled from his mouth and moaned.

"Oh, God, it feels so good."

"I've got something that will feel even better." He pressed her against the tile wall under the main spray of the shower. The other showerheads continued to hit their bodies, making their skin slick.

He held her gaze as he pushed between her wet folds. J.J. lowered down, taking him in. They both moaned and then pressed their foreheads together.

"God, you feel like heaven." His arms wrapped her tightly as she lifted up and thrust back down while holding on to his shoulders and head. His mouth was against her upper breast and he took the opportunity to lick and suck her skin. The water flowed between them as he began to make love to her, thrusting his cock deeper on every stroke. The water splashed between their bodies and soon he was pounding into her, trying to relieve his need to have all of her.

"Oh!" she moaned, tilting her head back, exposing her throat. The bruising tugged at his heart, a need to protect her from future harm feeding his inner ego. He'd never loved a woman before. Never cared for one so much that he wanted to wrap her in armor and keep her hidden from the world so that he would never lose her. With J.J. the thoughts came rushing through him on every stroke of his cock in her cunt, and every moan of pleasure from her lips.

They were both moaning and thrusting. Her nails dug into his shoulders and then she kissed his mouth, plunging her tongue inside and muffling his moans. He grew harder and penetrated deeper as she widened her legs and stuck her heels into his ass. He moved a hand over her ass cheeks and then pressed a finger to her anus. She bucked on his cock and he held her tight in his arms and snug against the wall.

He stroked deeper while his finger thrust into her ass and she screamed her release. Two more thrusts and he was on his way to exploding inside of her when she pinched his nipple.

"Fuck!" He roared and then pounded again and again as he lost it inside of her.

Holy shit. Their woman was filled with surprises. And yes, she was their woman.

He grabbed her face and kissed her mouth. She grabbed him back, covering his hands with hers as the water continued to spray them. He released her lips and stared down into her eyes.

"You are incredible."

She smiled and then she hugged him, and he never thought a hug could feel so right and fill such a gap in his heart that he had trained himself to ignore. She was special, and he would do everything in his power to prove it to her.

Chapter 6

Commander Frank Reynolds held the revolver in his hand. He knew that someone was in his home. He sensed it, as he called it into the department, directly to those he trusted. He had just finished showering and was getting ready for bed. It had been a long day downtown in the FBI headquarters. The few agents he trusted along with some detective friends were there too. He was the only one who knew where J.J. was, and that information was going to stay with him.

Frank called in his own team of friends and agents he trusted, as well as Sandman. It seemed that Sandman and his buddies knew a lot of people. Information was piling up on Congressman Dooley and the McCue brothers.

He heard something coming from downstairs. He slowly made his way down there, as the sounds of sirens could be heard in the distance. There was a crash to the right at the bottom of the stairs and he turned to see the man with the gun. The man fired a shot, and it missed Frank as he ducked and rolled then took two shots at the masked man. One hit his shoulder the other hit the wall behind the guy.

"Freeze right there, asshole," Frank stated.

The guy ran toward the window, and as he crashed through it, Frank fired his weapon again.

He ran toward the broken bay window and saw the masked man lying over the bushes. Glass was everywhere as the police showed up. He turned around in time to see why the man had broken into his home.

The old chest of photographs was spewed about the floor. Pictures of J.J. with Anthony, and some with him and other friends. There was a knife stuck into the coffee table along with a note. Frank moved closer. His breath caught in his throat as the police entered the home. There was a note and a picture.

Give up Jacobs, or this one is next. There was a picture of Frank's lover, Janelle, a detective in the police department and a friend of J.J.'s. They had been dating for months and were trying to keep it under wraps. He panicked as he pulled out his cell phone. He called her immediately as a few of his friends arrived on scene. He held up his finger and pointed to the table. They looked at it and then at him, as the phone kept ringing, but Janelle didn't answer.

Finally, right before he was going to hang up or let it go to voice mail, he heard her voice. "Janelle, where are you?"

"I'm out with friends. What's going on?"

"Someone broke into my home."

"Oh, my God, are you okay?"

"Yes. I need you to get over here right away. Are you carrying?" he asked her.

"What do you think?"

He smiled. "That's my girl. Be on alert. I'll fill you in when you get here."

"Oh, shit."

"Exactly. Get here and be careful."

"I got it."

He disconnected the call.

As he looked around the room, and at all the pictures in the chest, he knew that someone close to him had given a tip about that chest and about Janelle. But who? These guys were getting desperate. They'd probably found out about evidence piling up against Congressman Dooley. He was going down. They just needed a little more time. Now he wondered what he was going to do about Janelle. At least J.J. was safe, and no one would find her out there.

Hell, this guy was ready to kill him if necessary. It seemed that Frank might be in some need of protection now, too.

* * * *

J.J. held the towel around her body. She had taken a few minutes to dry her hair while Brook went to get some clothes.

As she looked in the mirror, she saw the red marks on her breasts and little love bites along her skin. They stood out more than the bruises and she smiled. Calder, Brook, Conway, and Lincoln were amazing lovers. She blushed just thinking about what she'd done with them. She was lucky to have been placed here with them, and not with some other people that weren't trustworthy. When she thought about that, she felt the bit of anxiety hit her gut.

She had conditioned herself to trust no one. Being an undercover officer meant relying on yourself and what you knew from seeing it with your own eyes. Gut instincts played a huge role in her job, and if she had truly been listening to her gut instincts that night at the casino, she would have declined the offer to have dinner with the McCues. But that was why she was there. She needed to infiltrate the organization and decipher who the rapists and killers were. Marlee, Denise, and even Tara had died horrible deaths. J.J. closed her eyes and thought about Tara and the scene that had unfolded before her.

Did Marlee suffer the same thing? Had Dooley raped her, played out his fantasy act, and then slit her throat? All while others looked on, laughing, enjoying their drinks and their own women? It made her sick. She could have died there in that room. Dooley could have chosen her. The McCues could have sexually assaulted her right at the table, with hands between her thighs and nowhere for her to escape. As she thought about it now, it almost felt like a movie, and she was watching everything happening. Yet, she felt it all, too. She felt the strange, male fingers pressing her thighs apart. The only protection was the dress she wore, but even that failed to protect her from their touch. They were going to make her go up to their room. *They're going to rape me.*

"J.J.?"

She heard Conway's voice just as she saw him standing in the doorway watching her. His expression was dark, his arms crossed in front of his chest. He looked upset. She swallowed hard.

"I'm all done," she said and placed the dryer under the counter, but before she stood back up, Conway pulled her into his arms.

"How many times did I say your name?" he asked her.

Her eyes widened. Had she truly zoned out entirely and not heard him? But hadn't he just appeared?

"J.J."

"Once," she whispered.

"No. I called your name several times."

"No. No you didn't. The dryer was on. I must have not heard you."

"The dryer was off. It had been for a few minutes. We waited, thinking that you were coming out to the bedroom, but you didn't come," Brook added as he showed up in the bathroom now, too.

"So what? Why are you bothering me about this?" She tried to pull from Conway's embrace, but instead he hugged her tighter. He kissed along her neck, and his arms, like vise grips wrapped tightly around her waist.

"You spoke out loud," Brook stated.

She panicked. She tried to remember what she'd said, what her thoughts were.

"You said, they are going to rape me."

Her heart felt as if it dropped to her gut. She closed her eyes and stopped fighting Conway. He lifted her up, and she straddled his waist despite the towel nearly falling from her body. She didn't want to open her eyes. She didn't want to share any information with them. She couldn't.

Conway sat down on the edge of the bed, and she saw Lincoln and Calder standing there, dressed in jeans, no shirts or socks. Their hair looked damp from their showers. She lifted up and grabbed the towel before it fell.

"I should go get dressed," she whispered.

Conway caressed her back with his hands. The towel fell and he stared at her.

* * * *

Conway had a thousand different scenarios going through his head and none of them were pretty. Had J.J. been raped? Is that what happened to her? It didn't seem possible with the way she gave herself to them with such passion and desire. He thought about the war in Afghanistan, and being stationed in different areas to come into the villages and capture potential terrorists and bombers. Sometimes he and his team showed up in villages that were raided by terrorist groups looking to put fear in the villagers. They raped the women, killed men and even children. It was horrific.

"I want to know what you meant by saying that. If we did something to bring back some memory—"

"No. No, Conway, I wasn't raped," she stated firmly and then held his gaze and pulled her bottom lip between her teeth. He was going to push but her expression appeared like she was about to respond.

"I really don't want to talk about it."

"Maybe you should, J.J.," Brook stated, and then sat down on the bed. Calder and Lincoln came over too and Calder sat on the other side of Conway.

"It might help if you talk about what happened to you. Obviously it was traumatic," Calder added.

She shook her head and tried to get up again. Conway pulled her snugly against him.

"Please, Conway. I don't want to talk about any of it. I'll deal with this."

"No. You've been dealing with it on your own now for weeks, probably even before you arrived here. We can help you," Calder said as he reached up and caressed her cheek. Her eyes glistened with unshed tears.

"I'm used to taking care of things alone. It's better this way."

Conway immediately felt angry. "How can you say that, after what we just shared? We care about you and want to help you any way we can. Seeing you in pain, or feeling alone, is upsetting."

"Conway, it has to be like this."

"No. It doesn't. What will get you to trust us, and accept that we have deep feelings for you? What?" Lincoln asked, raising his voice.

She looked at them and shook her head.

"I don't know. I just can't let my guard down."

"It's the training. You've worked undercover for years. You have to rely on your gut instinct and your own experiences to survive. You're stuck in survival mode," Conway said, and her eyes widened in surprise.

"How do you—"

"The war, being Special Forces, and all the shit we experienced. You think it was easy to become civilians again?" Conway asked her.

"Why do you think we take on special requests, like watching over people with bull's-eyes on their heads?" Calder asked as he caressed her forehead with his thumb. She shook her head and smirked.

"I don't know. Maybe you like whisking the unknowing scared females off their feet and into your lair? You know, seduce them with your muscles and charms," she teased.

"You're not an unknowing female," Conway sated.

"Nor some damsel in distress," Brook added.

"No other woman has ever been in this room, and we've never shared one woman together like we did with you," Calder stated very seriously.

She held Calder's gaze and nibbled her bottom lip again.

She seemed to be thinking about what they were saying. She closed her eyes and leaned her forehead lightly against Conway's chin as she rubbed her hands toward the back of his neck to hold him tight.

"If I'm going to explain what happened, I'd like to be dressed."

"Why is that? I kind of thought we would keep you just like this," Conway teased and then cupped her breast making the towel fall away from her body further.

She pushed at his chest. "Like that would happen."

"You disobey an order, ma'am, and a spanking or two may be in order," Lincoln teased, and Conway chuckled as J.J.'s cheeks turned a nice shade of red.

"Here. This is all you're getting. No excuses. We want to know what went down so we can help you," Brook said as he handed over one of Conway's T-shirts.

She looked at Brook.

"Panties?" she asked.

"I don't think you'll ever see any again around here," Calder stated, and she shook her head as she began to pull the T-shirt on, and Conway, Lincoln, and Brook chuckled, but Calder kept a very serious expression on his face.

* * * *

They each sat around the room. Calder and Lincoln were sitting on the bed, Brook in a chair he pulled over closer to the bed, and Conway held J.J. on his lap in another chair next to the bed.

Conway was caressing her thigh, under the shirt she wore, and she kept pushing his hand down.

"How am I supposed to concentrate with you doing that?" she asked.

"I can't help it. I enjoy touching you," he said, and she rolled her eyes and gave him one of her annoyed expressions he was getting to know so well. She wasn't all girly and dainty. She was strong and sexy, independent and capable. So why was his heart pounding as he waited with the others for her to tell her story? He feared what she would reveal. He knew whatever it was, it would make him and his team even more protective.

"So, was it your undercover job that landed you in the middle of this situation?" Brook asked.

"Yes. Uhm, just to give you a little background information, the local police department had investigated the disappearance of a young woman from one of the local casinos. A witness saw the woman leave with a male. Two days later her body was found."

"Damn," Conway stated. She looked at him and then continued.

"After a third woman went missing, the detectives had some tips that someone who either worked or hung out at this one casino was involved somehow. There was a certain type of woman that fit the profile, or so the investigators thought. They figured young, struggling to make ends meet, and trying to make some quick cash. The Nevada State Police has a program where they receive assistance from the federal government on cases involving crimes committed on or near casinos. With there being multiple murders, the feds stepped in. In the interim, Marlee went undercover."

"Marlee?" Calder asked.

J.J. looked away a moment and took a deep breath. Conway had a bad feeling in his gut. He had been over some things online with Sandman, who filled him in on part of this case she was talking about. They were guessing this was part of J.J.'s situation but they weren't certain. Conway was insisting on more information the more he and his team became personally interested in J.J.

"She worked in the same department that I did. She was really pretty, very gung ho about being a good cop. But she was new to the department and the force. The Commander thought she could ease her way into the casino and maybe get some inside information. But before she even got close, her identity was detected."

"What happened to her?" Brook asked.

J.J. got off Conway's lap and stood up. She nodded her head as she spoke, as if trying to act unaffected.

"She was raped, beaten, and murdered. We found her body way out in the middle of nowhere. It hardly even looked like her."

"That's awful, J.J. I'm so sorry," Lincoln stated. Conway reached out and pulled on her T-shirt.

"You were there when her body was discovered?"

"I was involved with this case along with the detectives. The agents sent one of their own in next, and she wound up dead. But instead of witnesses seeing Denise leave with someone from the casino, witnesses saw her leave, smiling and hugging some guy that we never found. They got into a limo, so we thought he had money and was maybe a regular. There wasn't too much to go by."

"So they couldn't get some guys in there as security or even maintenance workers?" Calder asked.

"No. It wasn't until I was asked to go in undercover in a completely different position than the others, because of my background. It was a huge risk, but some informants from the casino had said that some sort of illegal prostitution business was going on."

"What do you mean with your background? What was the position you had to fake?" Calder asked.

She took a deep breath and shrugged her shoulders.

"I was a Vegas showgirl. I had a stage name, wore sexy gorgeous outfits, and sang and danced. I was a huge hit, actually. The public responded to me so well and so quickly that I was noticed immediately."

"Wow, our own little sin city showgirl," Brook teased.

"That's impressive. You can't fake that kind of talent. You must be really good at performing and singing?" Lincoln asked.

"I had a lot of practice as a kid and in high school. I loved it. I probably could have gone professional maybe, but law enforcement was my calling."

"Why is that?" Conway asked.

"My dad was killed in the line of duty. My mom died during a convenience store robbery when I was thirteen. I guess I wanted to help stop criminals like that before they hurt or killed someone. I don't know."

"That's commendable, J.J.," Conway told her.

"Well, I fit the role, and I did such a good job that I attracted the men responsible for the murders."

J.J. began to explain about the owners of the club, the McCues, and then about how Tara approached her. She went on to describe the scene with Tara and the man in black who was acting out a role.

"Wait. Where were you when this was going on?" Conway asked.

* * * *

J.J. felt her body begin to shake and a chill run over her flesh. She clasped her hands together as she looked away from them. She walked over by the dresser and ran her hand across the carved wood. The furniture was absolutely stunning. She had never seen anything like it before.

"This furniture is gorgeous," she said, turning toward them.

"Brook made it," Lincoln told her and she was pleasantly surprised.

"Brook, you made this? You mean carved it by hand and everything?" she asked and he nodded his head. She was so impressed. What wonderful hands and a creative mind he must have to do such intricate work. She looked at him and held his gaze. He was so big and muscular up top. He had wide shoulders and those gorgeous brown eyes that more often looked sad than happy. She felt something inside her tingle like an awareness of some deeper emotion.

Then she thought about their question.

"Where were you when this guy was touching Tara and acting out some sort of game?" Conway asked her.

She turned back toward the dresser.

"I was caught between Martin and Dexter."

"Caught between them?" Calder asked.

She didn't look at them but continued to explore the room.

"I was escorted to a booth. Both men sat on either side of me. They talked about me earning extra money. I was focusing on their words and trying to decipher if they were in fact trying to get me to prostitute myself for them."

"Shit," Brook whispered.

"I heard the commotion going on across the room, and at first I thought the man was serious. Ya know, that he showed up and found his woman cheating on him. But nobody moved and when I asked Martin and Dexter if Tara was okay and thought that maybe I should help, they kept me where I was."

She didn't want to say how. Although something told her that getting this all out with them would be good for her.

"How did they keep you in place?" Conway asked, coming up behind her.

She gripped the dresser as he gently rubbed her back.

She pulled away.

"They held me by my inner thighs. They each used their hands to press against my thigh under the table."

"They touched you?" Conway asked.

She turned to look up at him. Standing at six feet four and filled with muscles, he was quite intimidating. She nodded her head and his eyes darkened.

She took a deep breath as she closed her eyes and then released it.

"Martin was stroking his fingers up and down against the material over my mound. He used his other hand to keep my hand over his crotch while the guy in black knocked over the other man and grabbed Tara, ripped her dress, and bent her over the table. Everything happened so quickly, and I couldn't move. When I tried they pressed harder." She was feeling her body shake again, and from there on out she rumbled through the story telling them everything about what happened next, and how they talked about taking her upstairs to their suite. She told them about Prentice, and how he went to check on Tara.

"What happened when they realized that Tara was dead?" Calder asked.

"The guy looked at me. He stated that the others couldn't handle him, and he had someone better in mind. He wanted me."

"What?" Brook asked, standing up.

"I–I can't tell you who the guy was. I can't. If I do then you're in as much danger as I am. He admitted to killing the other women. He said he killed them. That meant Marlee, Denise, and the others. It was some sick fetish he had about coming in and beating a woman then forcing himself on her over and over again. Those other women were forced to play a part."

"How the hell did you get out of there?" Conway asked.

"The guy recognized me."

"The killer? The one who just raped and killed Tara?" Lincoln asked, and J.J. gripped the dresser as she tried to keep the tears at bay. She wasn't a crier. Never had been.

"I said I felt like I was going to puke. They figured it was because of what I just witnessed. There were more of them than me, and the three undercover agents were in the surveillance room, so I needed to get to one of the cameras. I was nowhere near them. As soon as I started stepping away, the guy recognized me. I struck Dexter and took off down the hallway. I slammed through the exit and into the parking lot, but I still wasn't near the cameras. There was no backup, no one coming to help. I was all alone. I ducked down behind some cars to catch my breath and see if they were following. I figured I would grab a cab, you know, and get to the safe house. As I stood up and went to run, Dexter was there."

"What happened next?" Conway asked, staying right behind her as she held on to the dresser.

"These," she stated, pointing to her neck.

"He tried to choke you?" Calder asked.

"He nearly did, but I had a switchblade on me. I was holding it just in case and got it out of my purse. I stabbed him in the side with it. He struck me and I struck him back, and we fought. Hence the other bruises and then I took off. I ran and I got away."

Conway wrapped his arms around her from behind. She lowered her head to the dresser and absorbed the feel of his arms holding her.

"You were so brave, baby. So brave," he whispered.

"Who was the killer? Who could it be that you weren't safe in federal protection?" Calder asked as he approached.

She remained silent. She feared telling them. "It has to be someone important. Why else would feds take a bribe?" Brook asked.

"Tell us. Tell us so we understand and can help you get through this," Conway whispered as he squeezed her again. She turned in his arms and hugged him tight.

"I can't tell you. He wants me dead. He has more power and connections than anyone. My commander and the friends he has in the government and the Nevada State Police department are working on the evidence and building a case."

"But you're the eyewitness to a murder and his confession to the others," Brook said.

"That's why they want her dead. Who the fuck is this guy?" Lincoln asked.

"We need to know. We can't fully protect you if we don't know what we're up against. This is more than just you being a witness to a murder or testifying about a drug deal or something. This is way more serious, so tell us so we can help," Conway demanded.

"Who is someone in the spotlight, a public figure who loves and supports soldiers, police, and all first responders? Who's known all over the place as the guy who gets the job done even with all the red tape and bureaucracy? What position is someone like that in?" she asked.

"Sounds like a politician," Lincoln stated with his arms crossed in front of his chest.

She swallowed hard.

"What would you say if I told you that it was a politician? A congressman."

"Holy fuck," Calder said.

Conway placed his fingers under her chin and stared down into her eyes. She felt the tears fill up but not fall.

"Baby, is the killer a congressman? Is it Congressman Dooley?" he asked, and she widened her eyes and shoved away from him.

"You know him? You knew this all along. You work for him?" she asked in a panic. She was stepping farther away, and trying to head toward the door.

"No. No, I don't know him and we don't work for him."

She went to take off but Brook grabbed her.

"Calm down, J.J. We're not the bad guys. My God, you're so paranoid and distrusting. We care about you. We want to help you."

"You can't help me. Let me go. Oh, God, you know him. You know what he's capable of and how hard it's going to be to prove anything." She carried on until Lincoln placed his hands on her shoulders.

"He's a killer. It doesn't matter what his profession is or how much fucking money he has. He'll get caught, he'll be charged, and this will be behind you," Calder stated confidently.

She shook her head.

"It's not that simple. I witnessed him rape, beat, and kill Tara. He wanted me. He still wants me because now I stand to take everything away form him and destroy his life, his family, and his career. Everybody loves him. Even the feds were hitting walls as they tried to make the arrest and press charges. I was nearly shot outside of the precinct."

"What?" Calder asked.

"It's just a matter of time. Can't you see that? He's coming for me, and now that I told you, now that I'm here, he'll kill you, too."

Brook hugged her to him and held her head against his chest despite her attempts at pushing away.

"He won't hurt you. He'll never get his hands on you," Brook whispered.

"We're in this together. We can help, baby," Calder stated.

"We have our own very special connections," Lincoln said.

"Starting with Sandman and then with our closest friends and family. We'll help bring justice to those families and to you. We'll do it together," Conway said as he gently caressed her cheek.

J.J. didn't know if she could believe them or not. She wanted to. She didn't want to face all of this and her fears alone anymore. She wanted to give into the comfort of their touch, their embrace, and the power behind their words.

"I'm sorry that Frank got you involved with this. You were all living normal lives and then I come along and—"

Calder placed his hands against her face.

"And you walked into our home and our hearts. You're ours and we take care of what's ours." He kissed her, and she felt the tear roll down her cheek, and a little feeling of hope fill her heart. Perhaps these four American soldiers could save her from a fate she had already accepted.

Chapter 7

"Frank, explain it to us. This is a safe line. Conway's team helped to do their thing and make it secure. Isn't that right, Conway?" Sandman stated as he started the three-way conference call.

"That's right, Sandman. No one can listen in on this call. It's just you, me, and Frank. My men have been looking into the congressman," Conway stated.

"Do you really think that's a good idea? Every time the feds or some of the detectives start snooping deeper, we get a call or a threat. I just had one the other night," Frank told them.

"What happened?" Conway asked.

Frank explained.

"So you think they were just trying to scare you and that they would push for a location on J.J.?" Conway asked, and he tightened his jaw. He had become so protective of her. Every day, his attraction grew deeper.

"The incident shook me up. For one, they had a picture of my girlfriend, a woman I was seeing under the radar because she's on the job. So much for keeping that a secret anymore. The one who broke in was looking through old pictures of J.J."

"Why would you have old pictures of J.J.?" he asked.

Frank was silent, and Conway knew immediately that the man was holding back information. Was J.J. once his lover, too? Could she have had a fling with her commander? It was possible. Things like that happened all the time, and he was seeing a woman in the department, now. Conway pushed for answers.

"Well?" he asked.

"I've known J.J. for a long time. We're good friends. They must know this."

"There's something else that myself and Big Jay found out."

"A private investigator? You had Big Jay snoop around, too? Shit," Frank exclaimed, sounding really concerned.

"Hey, Frank, you can trust myself, my connections, and Conway's to be discreet. We're very good at what we do, and especially working as a team. Isn't that right, Conway," Sandman replied.

"That's right. We're pulling together our information and so far, we found that Dooley has been suspected of a lot of things. Things that if the public knew about, they sure as shit wouldn't reelect him," Conway stated.

"That's right. He's not such a supporter of the military either. He was involved declining military personal stipends and supplemental support upon their return from service to those who needed it. Then he tried to cover it up, by exclaiming that he and his constituents hadn't read all the fine print of the new law. A real shit, he is," Sandman said.

"We also found out that there were a series of incidents involving illegal prostitution. He would meet hookers at hotels, but not just any kind. He was into kinky shit. There was an investigation going on undercover as part of a sting operation. Drugs, manufacturing, and this illegal prostitution ring, where these thugs were bringing in women from other countries against their will. Anyway, an incident went down. There was gunfire exchange, a few undercover officers were killed, and Dooley was reported being at the scene. The specific information on that case was suddenly destroyed. It hadn't shown anything about Dooley being there," Conway told them.

"Where was this at, and when?" Frank asked, sounding upset.

"It was a couple of years ago. Out in Nevada. We have our men working on more and trying to uncover some of the buried information and possible evidence."

"Were the three men killed part of the special investigative unit here?"

"Yeah. One was the head of training," Conway said.

Again, Frank's silence was unnerving to Conway. He wished that he could see his face, read his body language, because then he might be able to tell if he was withholding information or hiding something.

"We'll keep digging. Conway and his men are very resourceful. They'll help nail this asshole."

"How is J.J.? Is she holding up okay?" Frank asked. Conway felt the jealousy immediately.

"She's tough and very smart. We're all getting along really well," he added, just to say it.

"Well, give her my best, and don't tell her about all this other stuff, like the break-in or the info on the murders and drug deal. She has enough to think about," Frank stated.

Conway immediately felt uneasy about Frank's remark.

"We told her that we would help her. That's what we plan on doing. The congressman's life is about to get a bit more unstable. Just keep calm. Do your job, and Sandman will be in touch if more is needed."

"Okay. I guess we really don't have any other options. Please, Conway. Keep J.J. safe. She's very important to me."

"He will. I'll be in touch," Sandman stated and then disconnected the call.

Conway leaned back in his chair and locked gazes with Calder.

"What do you think?" he asked him.

"There is or was something between them? J.J. and Frank, I mean. What do you think it?" Calder asked, as he leaned forward in his chair. He was wearing his camo pants and a black T-shirt.

"I'm not certain, but I think we should find out. Why don't you do your thing and start investigating Commander Frank Reynolds. Find out what you can and keep me posted."

"And what are you going to be doing?"

Conway turned around in his seat and started typing on the computer's keyboard.

"I am going to begin phase one of our plan. Let's see how the congressman feels about cyber harassment and losing some of his income to people who really need it."

"What are you going to do? Withdraw money from his account and transfer it to a secret account?"

"Nope. Out of the kindness of his heart, the congressman is going to donate a nice sum of money to each of the surviving families of the victims he killed. Simultaneously all his electronic devices will get an instant message that will broadcast to every single one of his contacts both public and personal."

"What is the message going to say?" Calder asked with a smirk.

"Oh. Something clever."

"How about give yourself up, you fucking loser?" Calder stated.

Conway chuckled.

"I think in this case, less is more. How about we start off with 'the truth will be revealed'? And then move on to listing the names of the victims under 'justice will be served'?"

"You better make sure this can't be tracked. I mean, even after we get this fucker behind bars and ensure that J.J. is safe. We don't need some bullshit charges against us," Calder stated.

"Calder, give me a break. I'm the chief of police. What the fuck do I know about computer hacking? Everyone in the office thinks I'm computer illiterate. That's more than twenty witnesses that prove I'm incapable of such things. Don't worry. You taught me well," Conway said and then typed away on the keyboard.

Calder chuckled.

"Phase one has officially commenced."

Chapter 8

J.J. and Brook were in his workshop. Brook was showing her some of the pieces he was working on and the different designs he planned on creating. As he worked on a new piece he was almost finished with, she looked it over. It was a gorgeous Texas mesquite cabinet, with multiple doors and an open area with crisscross wood that could hold about twenty-four wine bottles. The design on the top of the cabinet, in its rich mesquite and red cedar, caused streaks of unique patterns that were eye-catching and beautiful.

"I bet every piece that you make is different? The natural lines that the oils bring out are so bold and beautiful. You bring it to life," she whispered as he showed her how he glossed over the top of the wood after choosing the stain of his choice. The wood went from dull, but still beautiful, to absolutely gorgeous. She was impressed.

And as Brook explained more about his craft, she absorbed more of his work.

"Do you sell the things you make?" she asked. When she turned to look at him, he was running his large hands back and forth over the top of the wood as if checking for imperfections. He answered her. Something about a store in town and one in the city, but she was too busy staring at him. His eyes were focused on the wood and the direction his palms were going as he inspected it. The muscles in his forearms shifted and expanded with every stroke. Why she suddenly wished she were the piece of wood, she didn't know. But she did. She wanted his big, strong hands on her, stroking her, touching her, and bringing her that closeness and release she craved.

The black shirt stretched over his large muscles and she wanted to walk over to him, push her hands underneath the cotton material, and feel his skin against her palms. He was rock solid and so damn sexy, her panties were already wet from fantasizing about him.

He stopped what he was doing as if he realized that she was staring, and they locked gazes.

Holy shit. He is so gorgeous. His dark brown eyes held hers with such conviction and desire.

Then he squinted at her.

"Are you okay?" he asked, approaching, wiping his hands on his jeans. She didn't care if they had wood dust on them. She wanted them on her skin, against her breasts, bringing her pleasure.

He was in front of her, and the moment he reached out to place his fingers under her chin to tilt her face up toward him, she exhaled.

"J.J.?"

It was the scent of the fresh wood, the sawdust, his cologne and soap that hit her like a bolt of lightning.

She stepped closer and did exactly what she fantasized about doing. She found the hem of his shirt with unsteady hands, slowly pressed them against his waist colliding with the belt buckle, and then skin. His hard, muscular abs were warm to touch and she pressed harder as she moved up along his abs to his chest.

Gazing up into his eyes with her head tilted all the way back, she started taking uneasy breaths, and tears filled the back of her eyes. His scowl of concern just added to the attraction and need building inside of her.

"I want you," she whispered.

The dark brown of his eyes changed instantly from concern to excitement. She could have sworn she saw a twinkle right before he lifted her up and kissed her on the mouth.

She straddled his hips and held on tight as his hands moved everywhere. It was exciting, invigorating, and she didn't care where they were or where he placed her down, just as long as he filled her with his incredibly thick, hard cock pronto.

* * * *

Brook was feeling so sexually aroused just having J.J. in his workshop. But the fact that she seemed legitimately impressed with his craftsmanship touched his heart. She wasn't bullshitting. He would know. She saw things in the patterns of wood and his designs that not everyone noticed immediately. But what got him hot and heavy was her expression when he turned to look at her and saw the hunger in her eyes that matched the hunger in his body.

He was pressing his tongue deep into her mouth, wanting, needing to express the intensity of their connection.

He didn't know how he did it, but he pulled her shirt up and over her head, pausing only a second from kissing her to do it.

He used his hand to shove things off the worktable so he could set her down on it. The dust filtered through the air and he pulled from her mouth as he held her head between his hands.

"You drive me fucking wild," he told her.

The jade green of her eyes looked amazing and bright. They were filled with emotion and it appeared as if she were holding back tears. Could she be feeling the intensity he was feeling?

"I need you. Oh God, Brook. It's so crazy, but I want you so badly. Watching you work, using your hands to check the wood. I want your hands on me. I want you inside of me. Please, please, make love to me."

"Baby, you don't have to ask me twice. But it's kind of dusty in here. Maybe we should go inside."

She shook her head.

"I want you now. In here, with the scent of wood and all your hard creative work surrounding us. This is all you, and I want all of you," she said.

He covered her mouth and kissed her again. The feel of the palms of her hands moving up and down his chest and then to the waist of his jeans fired him up.

He pulled from her mouth and helped her to undo his pants. He pulled the condom from his pocket. He filled each pocket with one in hopes that she would feel the need to make love as much as he knew that he would want to. She had his heart already, and he'd fantasized about taking her in this room for weeks.

He pulled her down from the workbench.

"Turn around, bend over, and grab on to the wood for support."

Her eyes widened from his tone and he knew he barked out the order, but she did this to him. She turned him into a raving, wild man needy for her pussy and her pussy only.

Her delicate fingers collided with the wood. He reached around her and undid her jeans and shoved them down to the floor. The sight of her black thong panties made his dick grow another inch with anticipation. He ran his palms along each globe and she moaned.

"I love your ass, your body, your tits," he said as he smoothed his hand over the globes, around her ribs to her breasts, cupping them. She moaned, tilting her head up and her ass back. His cock was hard and between her ass cheeks.

"Fuck, baby, I want in."

"Get in then. Please, Brook. Please."

The desperation in her voice fed his male ego. She wanted him, needed him as much as he wanted and needed her.

He stroked a finger over her pussy and was pleasantly surprised to feel that she was hot and wet.

"Fuck, baby, you're soaked."

He kissed her neck and licked and sucked the skin.

She thrust back against him.

"I'm wet and hot for you, Brook. Please. Don't tease me."

She wiggled her ass again. He pulled back and gave her ass cheek a slap.

"Oh."

The sound of her enjoyment thrust him into action. He rolled the condom on, fisted his cock in one hand to align it with her cunt from behind while using his other hand to grip her hip, before he shoved in. He thrust to the hilt, making her moan and then push back.

He held himself within her. He kissed the back of her neck, her shoulder, and then cupped a breast. He pinched the nipple and she moaned.

"Inside you is heaven, baby. You feel like home, like warm fire in the middle of the winter, like a sunset on a beach after a storm."

He pulled out and then shoved back in.

"Oh, Brook. You feel amazing."

He continued to thrust into her, trying to ease the hunger and desire he had, but also the one J.J. had. Every time he pulled out to thrust back in, she countered, not giving him the time to move back in. She was desperate for his cock and that sent him over the edge.

He stared at her toned, muscular arms as she held on to the workbench. Her tan, gorgeous shoulders and muscular back. All the way down to her luscious ass. He was on fire.

In and out he increased his speed. He grabbed a hold of her ass cheeks, spread them, and then massaged them hard. She was moaning and panting, and he was focused on bringing her pleasure.

"You have one hell of a body on you, Vegas. I'm not ever going to let you go. You're mine now."

"Yes. Yes, Brook, please go faster, harder, I need it." She egged him on and that was it. He cupped her breasts and pounded into her cunt from behind while he pinched and pulled on her breasts. She was moaning and he was grunting trying to get deeper. He pulled his hands from her breasts to her shoulders and tightened his hold, as he ground deeper, as deep as he could get until he heard her scream her release and then he followed, moaning her name. He thrust three more times and then held himself deep within her, and relished in the aftermath of their amazing sex. The wood smell filled his nostrils. The scent of her perfume and shampoo encased them. He hugged her as he kissed her neck, her cheek, and then found her mouth, as she turned sideways.

They laughed against their lips at the awkwardness of their bodies in this position.

"Incredible," he whispered.

"You sure are," she replied.

"I was talking about you." She blushed and looked away. He squeezed her as hard as he could without hurting her before he slowly pulled from her body.

He turned her around and cupped her face between his hands.

"I meant what I said. I'm never gonna let you go, J.J. Never." Her eyes held his as he leaned down and kissed her.

He didn't tell her, but he knew instantly that he loved her. He loved her, and one day soon, he would tell her and hope that she loved him too.

* * * *

"I don't believe this. Look what Big Jay just sent me," Calder said to Conway, as he pulled off the headset and unplugged it from the computer. Lincoln and Conway were smiling and they looked happy. That had been a rarity until J.J. showed up at their home. That thought lifted Calder's spirits after the terrible video he'd just watched.

"What?" he asked and then Lincoln tilted his head toward the computer screen. Calder looked, and saw Brook and J.J. making love against his workbench.

He leaned back in his chair and watched a moment before Conway switched it off.

"She's incredible. I've never seen Brook so into anyone or anything but his woodwork," Lincoln stated.

"That's because the woodwork has been his lifeline, Lincoln. Without it, the nightmares, the memories would be ruling his life," Calder said.

"She's amazing, and more than anything we ever expected. We need to get her out of this danger. I won't rest easy until that scumbag and his cohorts are behind bars," Conway stated.

"Well, this thing that Big Jay just sent me is more evidence against the congressman," Calder told them and then turned the computer screen so they could all see the screen. He took some time to explain Big Jay's investigation to them and what was on the tape, and where Big Jay got it.

"So if this surveillance tape was one of the only ones from this drug bust, how the hell did the congressman's people miss it?" Conway asked.

"Let's just say that Big Jay has some serious connections, both legal and illegal." Conway smirked.

"You mean black market shit?" Lincoln asked.

"Even better. He made some calls, met with some informants, and then by chance got a hold of this guy whose brother in law worked at the location where this drug operation and sex slave business was being run. On top of this tape. There are others. The congressman liked to be videotaped while he did the down and dirty."

"Do you mean like during sex? When he killed those women?" Lincoln asked, appearing disgusted.

"Not the killings from the casino that J.J. was at. No, the videos are just him getting off on the crazy sex he had with these women. The fact that he knew they were sex slaves, restrained against their will, and also seemed to be fronting some money for the masterminds behind the sex slave business, I'd say the congressman is up shit creek," Calder stated.

"Is Big Jay getting those tapes?" Conway asked, appearing very serious.

"He sure as shit is. I got five downloaded and copied right now, and there are more," Calder added.

"The sick fuck. When we present this case, and hand over this evidence to the correct people, we'd better be sure to have copies of everything. We can't risk a fuck up," Lincoln added.

"Back up a little bit. Are you sure about the sex slave business? In the casino, it was more like a prostitution ring. What gives?" Conway asked, sitting forward in his seat.

Calder nodded his head. "The casino was definitely offering prostitution. It seems that Dooley had a sick fetish about hurting women and causing them pain. He wanted to take lives, probably to feel more powerful than anyone else. He paid for those women in the casino to play a role, and he got carried away. I think when he did, he wanted more. He thought nothing of taking those women's lives," Calder told them.

"That sick bastard. I hate him. I really fucking hate that guy," Lincoln said.

"Join the club. Now, Calder, how does this coincide with that video from Big Jay? How did the congressman get to this point of not being satisfied with the kinky sex and move on to murder?" Conway asked.

"Well, here is my thought on the whole thing. I think he started off doing this other stuff, like this sex slave business and drug production, to help feed his adrenaline rush. Being high profile, it probably excited him, like most sexual sadists, to get away with this stuff right under the radar."

"Yeah, and if his bodyguards knew about his extracurricular activities, then they would go down, too," Lincoln added.

"They sure as shit would and we've got their names. We've got everyone who would be in the vicinity of Dooley at all times. They'll get theirs too. But what I think started it all was this video. He apparently was into the sex slave business, hence the recording we have of him raping and assaulting these female victims in Nevada.

That night that the raid happened and the three officers were killed along with some women was captured on this tape. This tape alone can put Dooley away for a long fucking time. But there's more. Big Jay and Sandman are sending us files, with surveillance pictures and physical evidence that Dooley was involved with not one, but three illegal sex slave businesses, as well as his own little fetish of raping and killing women," Conway stated.

"What?" J.J. asked as she and Brook stood in the entryway. Brook was holding her hand and had his other hand on his shoulder as he stood behind her.

Calder thought they both looked happy and content. But this new information and this video were intense. He was thinking that perhaps Conway should see it and then decide if J.J. should. Calder was feeling overprotective of her.

"Hey, there you two are. We didn't know where you went off to," Conway said.

J.J. placed her hands on her hips and gave Conway a look.

"Sure you didn't. You know where I am all the time," she replied.

Conway curled his finger for her to come closer. She did without hesitation and that made Calder smile. One look at Brook and Lincoln, and they were smiling, too.

Conway pulled her between his opened thighs and placed his hands on her ass. He squeezed and she grabbed on to his shoulders.

"Don't get all sassy with me. Come down here and kiss me," Conway commanded.

She bent down and kissed him and he pulled her into his arms. When he was through kissing her thoroughly he smiled up at her.

"Enjoy making love in the workshop?"

Her cheeks blushed as she turned away and gave him a light smack to his shoulder.

He tapped her ass as she stood up only for Lincoln to wrap an arm around her waist and pull her against him. He kissed her next and then held her in front of him as Calder smiled.

"I'll get mine later. Right now, we have some updates for you," Calder told her.

"Updates?" she asked, stepping from Lincoln's hold.

"Yeah. Friends of ours have been very helpful in gathering some evidence that's been buried by the congressman. Calder just got a video of one of the sex slave operations the congressman was involved in."

"I think we should look it over first before she sees it, Conway. I don't know what's on it," Calder lied. He'd already seen the video and the murder of three officers trying to save their team's lives and the lives of the victims.

"Hey, I don't need to be censored here. I've seen my share of heavy shit, Calder. I can handle it."

He raised one eyebrow at her and she raised hers back.

"One spanking coming up," he whispered. Her cheeks flushed and she stepped back, only for Lincoln to wrap her into his arms again.

"I'm in on that. She could use a nice spanking and then a good, long, hard fucking," Lincoln whispered against her neck as he thrust his hips against her ass.

The others chuckled.

Calder locked gazes with her. "Later," he promised and she swallowed hard.

* * * *

J.J. couldn't believe it, but she was aroused and hungry all over again. Calder had such a way about him, with his authoritative, take-no-shit attitude. She loved it. And then there was Lincoln. Naughty, dirty talking, tattoo-covered Lincoln. *Holy shit, did he wet my pussy.*

She felt like a walking sex goddess. Like she could grab any one of them when she wanted, rip off their clothes, and have her way with them. She wanted to now. Right now in this cramped little space of a surveillance room with four large men and her.

It was so damn hard to concentrate on Conway's words as he explained what they had been up to. It wasn't until Calder mentioned the video that their friend Big Jay had scrounged up for them that she refocused. Something about the description of a crime scene, a drug bust, Congressman Dooley covering it up, and the murder of three cops. *A cop killer, too? The congressman had no limitations.*

It got her blood boiling and her heart racing. Then she saw the scene unfold on the computer screen. It was when she saw the sign, outside of the building in Nevada, that she nearly gasped aloud.

It can't be. Oh, God, please don't let it be. Oh, God, please.

She felt herself grip the chair she was sitting in. She glanced at the others. They were all watching the screen, all on edge as they knew the end result was three dead cops, some innocent female victims of the sex slave business, and countless others injured. She saw Dooley, and the sight of him made her shake. Someone placed their hand on her shoulder.

She turned quickly to the right. It was Conway. They locked gazes and his expression was firm, yet comforting.

She heard Dooley's words. "Kill them. Get rid of who you can, and burn the rest of it. Now," he ordered.

"But there are cops, too," the guy, she didn't recognize stated.

"Kill them. Who gives a fuck."

She covered her mouth with her hand. She held her breath as the video continued. "This is kind of intense right here. You can see the guys come out and take out the three cops. They never knew what hit them," Calder stated, as he looked at J.J.

"Maybe you shouldn't watch this," he suggested to her.

"I'm fine," she whispered but she wasn't fine. This was Anthony's murder. This was how her fiancé had died in the line of duty. Dooley was responsible for it. She knew the name on the sign. Rogers Industrial Park. Flashes of Anthony's face filtered through her mind. She would never forget his face. What he looked like alive and well.

Why am I watching this? Why? The video is going to show him getting killed. Oh, God.

She watched in horror as Anthony and his team walked right into the trap. Women were screaming for help. They were coming to their aid trying to get to them to save them. He knew there were victims in there and he was doing his job.

She saw them turn, the team of three and another set of four a distance behind them.

She knew it was Anthony. His stance, his body language, even in undercover clothes. The shots rang out. A series of *pop, pop, pop* filtered through the air. They hit him. He threw himself in front of his men, taking the initial blows, trying to protect them. But the rapid gunfire continued, until all three men were down on the ground and others were yelling and firing back.

Anthony. Oh, God, Anthony, you were so brave. You put yourself in the line of fire to try to save your men. Oh, God. Dooley killed you. Dooley is responsible for all of this.

"Baby? J.J., honey, can you hear me?"

Conway. What am I going to do? How do I explain this to them?

"J.J.?" Calder raised his voice.

She locked gazes with him. He looked so upset, and she realized that the tears were rolling down her cheeks.

"We shouldn't have let her watch it. Maybe it brought back memories of the incident?" Lincoln stated from the side of her.

"Fuck. She's not even responding," Conway stated.

She jumped up.

"I'm okay. I'm okay," she said and tried to flee the room. She just needed a few moments to organize her thoughts, to face and accept what she'd just seen. There was rage, anger, sadness, regret, and so many different emotions running through her system. She wanted to cry out in agony for her loss. She loved Anthony, but she couldn't do that, show that in front of these men. Calder, Conway, Lincoln, and Brook would be insulted, upset, or even angry with her. She didn't know. She was too scared to face it to tell them. Calder grabbed her by her arms and gave her a shake.

"J.J. Snap out of it and talk to us."

She looked up into his eyes. He was pissed off already.

"I can't. Not yet. Please. Not yet."

She hugged him and he hugged her back. She knew she'd probably confused him and she was buying herself time. Time to tell them that she had been engaged to Anthony, had been in love and that he had died. It was him being killed in that video and Dooley was responsible. She felt hatred. So much hatred and disgust for the congressman. She wanted to kill him. With her bare hands, with a gun, with anything she could get her hands on, just make him suffer.

She was crying hard against Calder's chest, and then he was carrying her out of the room.

It hit her all at once. As Calder sat down on her bed, with her standing between his legs. She looked at the others. All concerned, all angry. And she said the first thing that came to her head.

"I'm going to kill Congressman Dooley. I don't care if I die in the process. He's going to die, and I'm going to kill him."

Chapter 9

Dooley downed another glass of scotch as he stared at the computer screen. They were getting worse. Someone had hacked into all his computer programs, his cell phone, his contacts, and were spreading these pictures of him and words accusing him of rape, murder, and being a cop killer. They were popping up everywhere. People were calling him, and his own security team and computer people couldn't figure it out.

He felt the warm liquid burn down his throat. He was done, finished, and it was all that little bitch's fault. Where the fuck was she hiding out? Who was helping her to do this to him? If they knew about the video tapes, and they knew about the murders and had evidence, how could he stop them?

He was shaking with anger. He couldn't even call the McCues. They were picked up by a group of CIA agents, none of which were loyal to Dooley, and they were being charged with numerous crimes, including prostitution. He was next. At any moment they were going to come to that door and take him away. All his crimes, all his pleasure would become public record. If that bitch thought she was going to get the last laugh, she was wrong. Dead fucking wrong.

He picked up the phone and made the call.

"Do it. Take Reynolds out. This is the last thing I'll ask of you." He didn't listen to anything else. His guy would handle it. He'd kill Reynolds and leave that bitch with nothing, no one. See how she liked that.

* * * *

"She clammed up. She won't talk to any of us. What the fuck is going through her head?" Lincoln asked as he paced the kitchen. Brook was making a pot of coffee. It was just giving him something to do.

"Something isn't right. It was a difficult video to watch, but she seemed so intense and emotional over it. Was it just because Dooley was responsible? Was it because of her loyalty as a police officer? What?" Lincoln asked.

"Let Conway figure it out with her. We've got more bad news, and considering how J.J. feels about Reynolds, she might just lose it," Calder stated as he stood in the doorway. His hands were on his hips and Brook thought he looked really upset.

"What is it?" Brook asked.

"Yeah, what the fuck now?" Lincoln asked.

"Reynolds was shot outside of the police department. They don't know if he's going to make it," Calder told them.

"Oh, fuck," Brook said then looked toward the bedroom.

This was a nightmare in itself.

* * * *

"So you're going to sit there and not fucking talk to us?" Conway asked J.J. as she sat on the small windowsill and looked out toward the fields.

"I said I needed a little bit of time. There are a lot of crazy thoughts going through my head. There are things I need to tell you. I'm just trying to digest everything."

"Well, fucking digest it faster. I'm about this close to throwing you over my knees and spanking that ass. You don't know how to take an order for shit. How fucking long do you think we'll wait before we lose our fucking patience?

She glared at him.

"Sounds to me like you've already lost your patience."

He stepped closer.

"Tell me why you reacted the way to did to that video. What have you not told us about this case, your life, and what's going on? God damn it, J.J., we care about you, but you're making this very difficult."

"Conway, have you ever been in love?" she asked him and he was shocked. He blinked at her, felt his heart racing. She was fucking serious.

"No. I served too many tours in the military to commit to someone like that."

She looked at him with her hands clasped on her lap and her shoulders pushed back as if she needed that for confidence.

"How about you?" he asked, as he walked closer.

"Yes. I was engaged to get married," she said, and absently ran her fingers over her bare fingers where perhaps an engagement ring once sat. He didn't know how he felt about that. He knew he cared for her a lot. Hell, if he wasn't such a hardheaded bastard, he'd admit that he loved her right now.

"You were?" She nodded.

"What happened?" he asked, placing his hand on his hip as he stood right in front of her.

"He died."

"Ah, hell."

"Yeah, in the line of duty," she said, and then wiped her eyes before another tear could fall.

"Shit, baby, no wonder it was so difficult to watch that video," he said and then placed his hand on her shoulder.

She stood up, causing his hand to drop. She shook her head.

"His name was Anthony. He was my training coordinator, my commander for undercover work."

"How did it happen? How'd he die?" he asked her. Conway stared at her face. She tried to be strong as she stood there and her lip quivered despite her attempt to bite it from moving.

She locked gazes with him, as the tears poured from her eyes.

"You saw the video. That's how he died." She tried to muffle the cry but she couldn't, as he put two and two together.

He grabbed her by her shoulder to face him.

"That video we watched, Anthony was one of the officers killed?" he asked and she nodded her head.

"Oh, God," Conway heard from the doorway as he pulled J.J. into his arms and hugged her tight, while Calder, Lincoln, and Brook entered.

Conway was shocked. He was furious, he was numb, and all he could do was hold her as she cried. He couldn't even imagine what this was like for her. When was the pain going to end? When would she no longer suffer from any of this?

"I've got you, baby. God, I've got you," he said and then lifted her up and carried her to the bed. They lay down together, and he held her against his chest as he caressed her back. The others joined them, eyeing him with concern and lots of different emotions in their eyes.

Conway felt responsible. He should have found out more about that video and who was on there.

J.J. pulled back.

"I'm so sorry. I don't mean to cry. I'm not a crier," she stated as she wiped her eyes and tried to sit up. He pulled her back against him.

"Baby, don't be foolish. This is a terrible, scary situation. You've been through so much and then we just made things worse for you. My God, I'm sorry, J.J. So sorry," he said and then hugged her again, as he caressed her hair.

He felt her lips against his neck. She was kissing him, sucking along his skin, and then she climbed on top of him. She held his gaze as she sat above him. Eyes watering and red lip quivering.

"I need you. I feel so safe when one of you is inside of me. I feel no pain, no heartache, only love. Please, Conway, can you just love me, for now?" she asked. He reached up and cupped her cheek and neck as he stared at her.

"I love you already, baby. I've never said those words to any woman before. I mean it with you."

She lowered her mouth to his and kissed him.

* * * *

J.J. Pulled back from kissing Conway and lifted her shirt up and over her head. She felt fingers at the clip to her bra, glanced behind her, and saw Calder.

"Let's do this right, baby. We need you, too," Conway stated.

Calder lifted her up as her bra fell from her chest, and Conway stood to undress. She turned around to find Calder, shirt off, pants semiundone, and she reached up to kiss him. She pressed her breasts against his chest and squeezed him to her. Hands were on her waist from behind, unfastening the button on her jeans and pushing the material down her thighs.

She moaned into Calder's mouth.

"Here, condoms," Brook stated behind them.

Conway lifted her up backward. She was over his thighs, facing away from him, and he used his thighs to spread her. She felt the cool air hit her pussy and then Calder bent down and pressed a finger to her pussy.

"You're so fucking sexy. The way you took charge of Conway and attacked him on the bed. I can't wait to fuck this sweet, wet pussy," Calder told her and then leaned forward and licked her cunt.

Conway spread his thighs wider, giving Calder full access to her ass and pussy.

She leaned back against him, and he cupped her breasts as his cock pressed against her back.

"You smell so good," Conway said and kissed her mouth as she turned toward him to catch his lips with hers.

She moaned into his mouth as Calder thrust two fingers in and out of her cunt. When his fingers moved, his mouth replaced them, and then she felt him move the wet digit to her anus.

"Relax that ass, baby, it's about to be filled with cock," Calder said and she pulled from Conway's mouth and screamed her first release.

"That's it. Come on," Conway demanded.

In a flash she was lifted up and turned around. She grabbed on to Conway's thighs and watched as he encased his long thick cock with the latex. He must have gone too slow for Calder because a hand pressed her back down and then Calder thrust his cock into her pussy from behind.

"Fuck!" he yelled out.

She gripped Conway's thighs and saw the intensity in his eyes.

"I need her," Conway whispered, as he cupped her cheek and caressed her lower lip with his thumb.

"I was just keeping her pretty little pussy wet and ready for us, bro," Calder teased and then pulled out of her cunt.

She climbed up onto Conway and took his cock into her swiftly, needing the connection so badly it burned in her gut.

Up and down she eased him deeper, holding on to his shoulders and thrusting downward.

Behind her she knew that Calder was getting her ready for his cock. First came the cool liquid and then his thick, hard fingers.

"Oh God. Oh!" She moaned.

A moment later he was kissing her neck and shoulder.

"I love you. I've never told a woman that ever and don't plan on telling anyone but you." He nipped her ear and pressed his cock through the tight rings of her ass binding his proclamation.

"I love you, too, Calder. Oh, God, I love all of you," she stated.

The bed dipped and she felt the hand by her cheek and there was Lincoln. He was naked and holding his cock in his fist and looking ready to explode.

"I need you. I need that hot wet mouth on this cock, right now, woman."

"Yes, sir," she said, and then gasped as Conway and Calder thrust into her hard. She leaned down lower to adjust to the position to be able to suck on Lincoln.

She opened wide and accepted the thick, hard muscle and began to lick and suck what she could reach.

In and out Calder and Conway continued to thrust into her and make her body tighten like a bow.

She felt Calder's hands on her hips and him grip her hard before he stroked into her ass four more times very deeply.

"J.J.!" He roared and then shook as he exploded inside of her.

She moaned, losing her hold on Lincoln's cock as she felt her body begin to come. Conway grabbed her hips and together they moved in sync until he came and she followed.

She was gasping for air when she looked at Lincoln and Brook. She opened her arms.

"I need you both," she said.

Conway pulled on her nipple making her gasp. She swatted his hand away and he rolled her to her back, and then slowly pulled from her body. He leaned down and kissed her belly. "I'll be back," he said and winked. Her heart soared.

Lincoln took position on the side of the bed and she immediately climbed onto him as he adjusted the condom into place. She leaned down and kissed him deeply, as his hands roamed over her ass cheeks and parted them.

"She's not wet enough," he stated.

"What?" She gasped and then felt the smack to her ass. She looked back and there was Brook, smiling wide, condom in place and a tube of lube in his hand. He shook it at her. "We know how much a good spanking will turn that pussy all wet and slick for cock."

"Oh God, take me." She moaned.

"With pleasure," Lincoln said and then aligned his cock with her pussy as she lifted up and pulled him in.

She began to ride him slowly, trying to ease that long, thick cock of his into her very tight cunt. It took a few strokes and then another three slaps to her ass and a finger full of lube to her puckered hole to send Lincoln all the way into her. She held still with a cock in her pussy and fingers stroking her ass and she moaned.

"Don't you come yet. We both need to be inside of you. That's where we belong," Brook said and then pressed her back down so she could straddle Lincoln's chest and spread her thighs wider.

Lincoln thrust upward a few times as Brook pulled his fingers from her ass and replaced them with his cock. She closed her eyes and relaxed her body, just as her four lovers had taught her. The feel of the mushroom top elicited a moan from deep within her and she craved that sensation of fullness.

"Please, Brook. Please." She moaned, sliding her hips up and down and slowly backward as she took Lincoln in and out of her cunt, and pulled Brook deeper into her ass. She felt the sensation and knew that Brook was all the way in and she smiled.

"That's right. Our woman loves two cocks in her at once," Lincoln stated.

Smack.

"Oh!"

"And a good spanking, too," Brook said and so it began. Brook and Lincoln worked in sync, thrusting, spanking, and stroking her cunt and ass until she screamed her release and they followed.

"We love you, baby. We're never gonna let you go," Brook said and then kissed her shoulder as she tried to catch her breath.

* * * *

Lincoln and Conway stayed in bed with J.J. as she drifted off to sleep. Calder went to check on Reynolds's status, whispering what had happened to Reynolds once they knew she was deeply sleeping.

Lincoln had just started to drift off, feeling content with J.J. in his arms, and with Conway there too. But then they both felt J.J. shaking and then they heard her moan. She was tossing her head, trying to push from their embrace.

"J.J., wake up. It's Conway and Lincoln," Lincoln whispered as Conway tried to brush her hair from her cheeks.

She jerked forward, with her hands on her throat and her eyes wide open. She was gasping for air.

"You're okay. You're safe. He doesn't have you," Conway told her and Lincoln felt like hitting something. He wanted to take away all her pain.

"Baby, it's okay. Just breathe," Lincoln whispered and she looked at both of them and then closed her eyes and lay back down between them.

They both leaned up on an elbow and placed a hand on her belly. They were staring down at her.

"Okay now?" Conway asked, as she opened her eyes, and she smiled.

"Oh, God, that wasn't too bad. Not too terrible at all."

"What?" Lincoln asked. He was upset. How bad were these episodes and how often did she have them?

His expression must have indicated his question because she reached up and cupped his cheek. She smiled softly.

"They're getting better."

"How so? It didn't look or sound good at all," Conway asked in that very demanding tone of his.

She reached up and touched his cheek, too.

"Despite the fear, I felt the two of you here with me. Your voices cleared my mind. I'm sure tonight is going to be hell. I think I'll need you both next to me, holding me just like this," she said and then winked.

They shook their heads at her.

"No more secrets. No more pretending that you're strong enough to handle shit on your own. You're our woman and we'll take care of you. Got it?" Conway asked.

"Got it, Chief," she replied sarcastically and Lincoln chuckled as Conway began tickling J.J.

Her laughter filled the room and his heart grew fonder of the woman instantly.

She reached for his forearm and pulled it around her waist, making Lincoln lean back down. His arm was now under her breasts, across her ribs, and she was tilting her ass back against his cock.

"Now. Let's try resting a little longer and then take showers."

"Sounds like an order to me," Lincoln reprimanded.

She moved his hand over her breast to cup at as she reached her other hand over to pinch Conway's nipple. "Hey."

"Hey yourself. It's not an order. It's a promise for more lovemaking in the shower."

Lincoln squeezed her breast and then leaned down and kissed her cheek. If only they could stay this happy, and in this peaceful, lighthearted moment forever. But they couldn't. Danger was too close, and another man may be dead because of the congressman. He squeezed her to him and closed his eyes, hoping they could keep her safe and be happy like this forever.

* * * *

"I have to see him. We're going. I don't care how, but I'm going to see Frank. When can we leave?" J.J. asked as Conway, she, and Lincoln joined Brook and Calder in the living room. They'd just told her about Frank, and that he was in critical condition, and that he had been shot.

"Whoa! You're not going fucking anywhere," Calder stated firmly.

"Didn't you hear what we just said? Dooley disappeared. He's on the run. He's a fucking wanted man, and he hired someone to kill Frank. That means he could have sent others to kill you," Lincoln added.

"You don't know that. You sent all the information to the feds and the people that your friends believe to be trustworthy. They're already raiding Dooley's office, confiscating his files, and going over all the evidence. Multiple people have been arrested and will be charged. We can head to Nevada. I can see Frank. I need to see him." She raised her voice.

"Why? Why the fuck do you need to see your commander? Can't you just let things fall into place? He wouldn't want you to come see him with your life still in danger," Conway said.

"I have to see him. He could die and then what?"

"You could die, J.J.," Brook added.

"You don't understand. Frank is the only family, the only friend and connection I have left."

"Connection to what? The fucking police department, the people who turned on you, what? Who?" Calder asked in frustration.

"To Anthony. Frank is all I have left of Anthony," she yelled back and then covered her face with her hands and then her mouth. They just stared at her.

"Explain," Conway stated in his very authoritative manner. She looked at him.

"Frank is Anthony's uncle. If he dies…"

Brook pulled her into his arms and hugged her.

"Fuck. This just keeps getting more and more complicated," he whispered.

"Hey, you're not alone. If something happens to Frank, or if Frank pulls through, either way, you are not alone. You have us now, and we have you," Conway told her as she pulled back from Brook. She looked at each of them.

"We need to go there. This has to come to an end. All our ducks in a row, all the evidence submitted, my testimony told, and it ends, forever."

The room was silent and then Conway spoke.

"Looks like we're heading to Vegas."

Chapter 10

When they arrived at the hospital, there were agents and officers providing security, and J.J. spotted Janelle. She walked over to her and they embraced.

"Oh, thank God that you're safe. Frank was so worried," Janelle stated.

"How is he doing, Janelle?" she asked, knowing that Janelle cared about Frank.

"He's a tough bastard. He's hanging in there. Every day looks promising. Why don't I take you up there to see him?" She placed her arm around her and then Conway stopped them.

"Whoa, where are you going?" he asked.

"I'll take her up," Janelle said.

"It's fine. That's Frank's girlfriend, and she's one of us," one of the detectives stated.

"Meet me up there," J.J. told the men and then headed toward the elevator with Janelle. They got in and J.J. saw that Janelle was carrying and was in that stance of hers she always did when she was getting ready for something. She was a good cop, and always in protective mode.

"Those guys are huge. Are you sleeping with any of them?" Janelle asked.

"What?" she asked, kind of surprised by the comment. Janelle pressed the button and the doors closed. As soon as the elevator started to go down instead of up, J.J. had a bad feeling. She stepped forward.

"I thought you said up? We're heading down," J.J. said.

"Oh, shoot, I must have hit the wrong button. Once we get down, we'll just hit the third floor."

"The third floor? Frank is on the fifth in intensive care," J.J. questioned.

"Always such the good detective. You're never wrong are you, J.J.?"

"What?" J.J. asked as Janelle pulled out her weapon and aimed it at her. J.J. gasped.

"What the hell?"

"Sorry, J.J., but I need money. I don't get paid shit being a cop. Plus you got Anthony. He was supposed to be mine. He liked you from the start and never even noticed me."

The elevator doors opened and J.J. saw the limo as well as Dexter and Martin standing by it.

"You did this? You fucking sold me out, your friend, your fellow cop, to a bunch of rapist killers?" she yelled.

Janelle shrugged her shoulders. "Payback's a bitch."

Janelle slammed the gun against J.J.'s temple making her fall to the ground.

Dexter approached. "You and I have some unfinished business." He started pulling her toward the limo as Martin approached.

"You're in for it, Jade. When we're through with you, they won't even be able to find all the parts."

"Let go of me," J.J. screamed despite the pain in her head and the blood dripping into her eye.

"Hey, where's my money?" Janelle asked.

"Oh, we lied," Martin said and then lifted a gun and shot Janelle in the head. J.J. gasped as Dexter attempted to get her into the car. She fought him hard, kicking him in the groin and then slugging him in the face. The gun fired again, she felt the pinch against her arm, and cried out.

"Get that bitch in here."

She realized instantly that she was hit and that the voice she heard coming from the limo was Congressman Dooley. The police were wrong. Sandman was wrong. Dooley wasn't where they thought. He was right here and he wanted her dead.

J.J. scrambled to run but Martin grabbed her by the hair and squeezed her arm where the blood dripped from the wound. She cried out and fell to the ground.

"Get her in here. We're running out of time," the congressman said as he stepped from the limo.

"Stop fighting it. I always win. You're not going to live after what you've done to me."

"You did it to yourself. You're a worthless piece of shit," she yelled and Martin struck her, making her fall to the ground. Dexter kicked her in the ribs and she swung her legs around fast across the concrete to take out Martin. His gun went flying as the doors to the stairway burst open. Sirens wailed as cars came screeching through.

"Die, bitch! Die for what you've done," the congressman yelled. She rolled and pointed the gun, pulling the trigger twice as the congressman pulled the trigger, too.

The bullets from his gun echoed against the concrete by her head. The congressman fell to the ground, bleeding from his throat and head. He tumbled to the ground as Martin and Dexter jumped toward her. Before they reached her, two large shadows pulled them back and threw them to the ground. Dexter and Martin were handcuffed by Conway and Calder as Brook and Lincoln fell to their knees next to her.

"Holy shit. Are you okay?" Brook asked.

"You're hurt," Lincoln stated as he gently moved her arm.

"Just a flesh wound. Is he dead? Did I kill him?" she asked.

Brook nodded his head. "The congressman can never hurt anyone again."

Chapter 11

J.J. was talking to Grace and Gia Marie at the bar, while the guys stood by their friends keeping a close watch.

"So, a Nevada State Police investigator, huh? You lucky bastards," Duke teased.

"Hey, maybe they're not so lucky. J.J. sure can handle herself. It can make a man, or men, feel inferior," Big Jay stated. They laughed.

"No way. She's gorgeous, she's smart, she can kick all your asses, and she knows how to handle a gun. I'd say we're pretty darn lucky," Lincoln said and then took a slug of beer.

"She can also sing and dance. At least that's what Gia told us," Sandman said.

"She sure can, but no one but us will ever see her dance," Calder said as J.J. walked over.

"Hey, what's going on?" she asked as she joined them.

Lincoln smiled as he tucked her next to him as she leaned her head against his chest. Her arm was in a cast and sling, after the bullet had lodged into the bone and cracked. She hadn't been a happy camper at all.

"Just talking about how you can dance. Lincoln was saying that you were a pole dancer," Big Jay stated and Lincoln widened his eyes right before the smack to his gut made him lose his breath. They all started laughing.

"Damn, J.J. They're messing around. I never said any such thing."

She looked at him and then leaned her head back against his chest. He held her firmly.

"Well, if you're going to go around telling everyone that I was a Vegas showgirl, you should get it right. I didn't always use a pole," she said and the hoots and hollers echoed around the room. Calder grabbed her hand and pulled her into his arms. The others moved away, leaving them with their woman as they still laughed.

Lincoln, Calder, Conway, and Brook gathered around J.J. Calder held her tight and put his hands over her ass cheeks.

"Hey," she reprimanded.

"Hey yourself. We own this ass," Calder announced loudly. More chuckles erupted.

"Now, what's this about you sometimes using a pole when you danced?" Lincoln asked her. She looked at him and smiled.

"Oh, wouldn't you like to know."

Conway tugged her hair, and she looked at him.

"Oh you're going to tell us, or you're going to show us as soon as we get home," he stated.

"Only if you're good boys, will I show you," she whispered and winked. The slap came to her ass quickly and she gasped and then another two landed firmly on her rear.

"Hey!"

They all kept a hand on her. Two on her ass, one on her shoulder, and another on her waist.

Calder held her gaze firmly.

"Oh, you will be showing us, and only us," he said.

"Really? I was kind of thinking about retiring from the force, and maybe giving the Vegas thing a real shot. You know, sexy sequin dresses where my breasts pour from the top, makeup, roaring crowds, men pressing money into my cleavage. I hear that the popular girls can make a few grand a night just from what's stuffed down their cleavage. I figured with my rack, I'll be set," she teased as she pulled gently on her shirt so more cleavage would show.

The men got angry but then Lincoln held her chin with his fingers and stared into her eyes.

"Oh, no, you won't be. You'll be too busy with us, rolling around on the mats in the dojo, bending over the workbench in Brook's workshop, laying spread eagle on the kitchen table for me. I'd say that our sin city showgirl is officially retired."

"Oh really?" she asked as she smiled, with her cheeks a nice shade of red.

"Really. Now let's head home. You've got about four punishments coming your way, and my hand is itching to start the first one right here and now," Calder stated.

"You wouldn't dare," she teased, as they were waving good-bye to their friends while shuffling her out the door.

Before the door closed Lincoln slapped her ass and she squealed.

"Come on, Vegas, we've got a hell of a night planned for you, and a heck of a ride home," Calder whispered as he trailed a finger over her jeans to her pussy making her close her eyes and moan.

"A girl's got to love an American soldier. You're all so damn sexy," she whispered and they chuckled as they climbed into the vehicle.

Lincoln smiled the moment he saw Calder pull J.J. onto his lap. She straddled his waist and kissed him deeply. Oh yeah, they were blessed. J.J. came into their lives filled with piss and vinegar and an attitude that rocked their worlds. Her heart was broken, her distrust torture, and she was exactly like the four of them. All alone, with only nightmares and memories to hold on to until now. They loved her just the way she was. Tough, bullheaded, and drop-dead gorgeous. Life didn't get any better than this.

THE END

WWW.DIXIELYNNDWYER.COM

ABOUT THE AUTHOR

People seem to be more interested in my name than where I get my ideas for my stories from. So I might as well share the story behind my name with all my readers.

My momma was born and raised in New Orleans. At the age of twenty, she met and fell in love with an Irishman named Patrick Riley Dwyer. Needless to say, the family was a bit taken aback by this as they hoped she would marry a family friend. It was a modern day arranged marriage kind of thing and my momma downright refused.

Being that my momma's families were descendents of the original English speaking Southerners, they wanted the family blood line to stay pure. They were wealthy and my father's family was poor.

Despite attempts by my grandpapa to make Patrick leave and destroy the love between them, my parents married. They recently celebrated their sixtieth wedding anniversary.

I am one of six children born to Patrick and Lynn Dwyer. I am a combination of both Irish and a true Southern belle. With a name like Dixie Lynn Dwyer it's no wonder why people are curious about my name.

Just as my parents had a love story of their own, I grew up intrigued by the lifestyles of others. My imagination as well as my need to stray from the straight and narrow made me into the woman I am today.

For all titles by Dixie Lynn Dwyer, please visit
www.bookstrand.com/dixie-lynn-dwyer

Siren Publishing, Inc.
www.SirenPublishing.com

Lightning Source UK Ltd.
Milton Keynes UK
UKHW02f1352160318

319572UK00006B/926/P

9 781627 413695